A Royal Engagement

Summoned for His Highness's pleasure...

Would you dare refuse a royal order?

Discovering that power, status and wealth can't
buy them love...these brooding aristocrats will
have to use the other weapons in their regal
arsenal...charm, seduction and a passion that will
shake their reluctant brides to the core!

Find out in **A ROYAL ENGAGEMENT** featuring
two passionate stories from
two *USA TODAY* bestselling authors,
Trish Morey and Caitlin Crews.

TRISH MOREY is an Australian who's also spent time living and working in New Zealand and England. Now she's settled with her husband and four young daughters in a special part of south Australia, surrounded by orchards and bushland, and visited by the occasional koala and kangaroo. With a lifelong love of reading, she penned her first book at the age of eleven, after which life, career and a growing family kept her busy until once again she could indulge her desire to create characters and stories—this time in romance. Having her work published is a dream come true. Visit Trish at her website, www.trishmorey.com.

Books by Trish Morey

Harlequin Presents®

*Dark-Hearted Desert Men

CAITLIN CREWS discovered her first romance novel at the age of twelve. It involved swashbuckling pirates, grand adventures, a heroine with rustling skirts and a mind of her own and a seriously mouthwatering and masterful hero. The book (the title of which remains lost in the mists of time) made a serious impression. Caitlin was immediately smitten with romances and romance heroes, to the detriment of her high school social life. And so began her lifelong love affair with romance novels, many of which she insists on keeping near her at all times. She currently lives in California, with her animator/comic book artist husband and their menagerie of ridiculous animals.

Books by Caitlin Crews

Harlequin Presents®

*The Notorious Wolfes

2 Stories in 1

Trish Morey
Caitlin Crews

A ROYAL ENGAGEMENT

Harlequin®

TORONTO NEW YORK LONDON
AMSTERDAM PARIS SYDNEY HAMBURG
STOCKHOLM ATHENS TOKYO MILAN MADRID
PRAGUE WARSAW BUDAPEST AUCKLAND

Recycling programs
for this product may
not exist in your area.

ISBN-13: 978-0-373-13028-3

A ROYAL ENGAGEMENT

First North American Publication 2011

The publisher acknowledges the copyright holders
of the individual works as follows:

THE STORM WITHIN
Copyright © 2011 by Trish Morey

THE RELUCTANT QUEEN
Copyright © 2011 by Caitlin Crews

CONTENTS

THE STORM WITHIN
Trish Morey

With grateful thanks to the real Archival Survival
team, Angela Henrickson and Geoff McIntyre,
and especially to Annie for all her help with a
project that was so totally left field.

I'm not sure if this is what you envisioned Annie,
when I first put the premise of this story to you,
but thank you so much for your advice and
assistance and for your sheer enthusiasm!
Any mistakes or omissions are purely author error.

Thank you Annie!

CHAPTER ONE

SHE was coming. From his office overlooking the sea, Count Alessandro Alonso Leopold Volta watched the launch approach the island that was home to Castello di Volta and the seat of the Volta family for more than five hundred years.

The boat hadn't even docked and already the bitter taste of bile hovered menacingly at the back of his throat.

He growled. He hated visitors, hated the way they brought the smell of the outside world with them, as if clinging to their very clothes. He hated their wide-eyed stares and their looks of horror when they first saw his scars, horror that bleached their faces white and sent their eyes skidding away to the floor or to the nearest work of art. Anywhere, it seemed, that wasn't his face.

But most of all he hated their pity, for the horror always gave way to pity.

He preferred the horror.

His hands curled into fists at his side. He didn't want anyone's pity.

He didn't want anyone. *Period.*

The launch slowed, rocking sideways on the bumpy water as it neared the dock and its wash caught up with it. He ground his teeth together and turned away, knowing that this time he had no choice. The package found tucked away in the caves deep beneath the castle had seen to that.

Why here? he asked himself again. Why, of all the places

in the world, of all the places that would welcome the attention such a discovery would bring, why had what could be the lost pages from the fabled *Salus Totus*, the legendary *Book of Wholeness*, had to turn up here? When had fate taken to wearing a clown's mask?

He grunted his displeasure and dropped into the chair behind his desk. One week Professor Rousseau had promised him the job would take. No longer than one week to examine and document the pages, to determine whether they were genuine, and if so to stabilise their condition until they could be taken away and prepared for display. One short yet no doubt interminable week, with a stranger clattering around the castle, asking questions and expecting answers, and probably expecting him to be civil in the process.

He looked down at the file he'd been reviewing before the onshore wind had carried with it the thumping beat of an approaching engine, but his skin pulled achingly tight over his jaw and the words before him danced and spun and could have been printed in a different language for all the sense they made.

It could be worse, he rationalised, clamping down on the rising black cloud of his resentment, forcing himself to focus on the résumé in his hands. He flipped the page, turning to the photograph of the woman he was expecting. Reputedly one of the best conservators in the business, Professor Rousseau boasted more than forty years' experience in the industry. And with short grey hair cut helmet-style around features that looked as if they'd been sculpted from parchment rather than skin, she looked the kind of person who enjoyed books more than people. If he had to put up with a visitor to his island, he could do much worse than this shrivelled-up scientist.

Maybe. And yet still this heavy sense of foreboding persisted in his gut; still the jagged line of his scar burned and stung, as if someone had dragged their nails down his face and chest and sliced open his wound.

One week, he thought, touching fingers to his burning cheek, half surprised when they didn't come away wet and sticky with blood. One week with a stranger poking around his castle, asking questions, getting under his feet. And whoever she was, and however she looked, it would be one week too long.

CHAPTER TWO

DR GRACE HUNTER TOOK a gulp of sea air and did her best to ignore the butterflies that had seized control of her stomach and were right now threatening to carry it away. Excitement, she told herself. Anticipation. Maybe a little bit of motion sickness too, given the way the launch bounced and lurched over the chop.

But excitement. Definitely there was excitement.

The *Salus Totus* was the Holy Grail, the Troy of the conservatorial world, and the plum job of examining the pages discovered had fallen right into her lap. If the pages were authentic, and indeed the fabled long-lost pages, if she could prove they were no hoax, her studies of it and the papers she produced on it could make her career.

She *should* feel excited.

And yet there was something else beneath the thrill of the chase. Something else lurking below the anticipation of holding a page written hundreds of years ago, of feeling that connection between writer and reader that transcended the centuries and rendered time meaningless. And that something else twisted in her gut until the butterflies turned into a serpent that coiled and squirmed in her belly.

Difficult, Professor Rousseau had described Count Alessandro Volta, during her unexpected and rapid-fire phone call from the hospital yesterday, and when Grace had asked what she meant there'd been a distinct hesitation on the line, before other muffled voices had intruded, and she'd added a rushed, 'I have to go. You'll be fine.'

Sure. She'd be fine. She gulped in air as the boat ploughed resolutely through the chop and headed for the relative safety of the shore. *Relative*, because nothing about the rocky island and the imposing castle set upon it looked remotely welcoming. Not the rocky shore or the towering cliffs or the clouds that seemed to hover ominously above the brooding castle in an otherwise clear sky.

She frowned up at them. Lucky she was a scientist, really, and not some paranoid panic merchant who saw portents of doom in every swirling cloud or flutter of apprehension. She was here to do a job after all.

The skipper cut the engines, letting the wash carry the boat into the dock, while the other crew member secured a line, taming the motion before starting to offload cargo onto the dock, her duffel bag amongst it. She gathered her things, her leather backpack and her briefcase containing the Professor's letter of introduction, along with her specialist tools, glancing up at the castle that sprawled so arrogantly across the cliff-top. From sea level the sheer scale of the place was daunting. Up close it must be intimidating, with its high walls punctuated at intervals by perimeter towers topped with crenellated battlements, a central tower rising high above it all, almost sending out a challenge—*enter if you dare*.

Welcoming? Definitely not. A movement startled her and she jumped as a figure unexpectedly stepped from the shadows thrown by the rocky escarpment into the bright sunlight. Through grizzled eyes in a leathery face the man looked her over as one might consider an unwelcome stray dog found whimpering on the doorstep, before he grabbed her duffel in one dinner-plate sized hand and flung it in the back of a rusty Jeep. He made a lunge for the briefcase in her hand and she pulled her arm away. There was no way she was letting Mr Sensitive loose on her tools.

'Thank you, but I'm good with this one.'

He grunted. 'You are not who we were expecting,' he said in gravelly English, his accent as thick as his ham-hock biceps, before he muttered a few words in Italian to the skipper and hauled himself into the driver's seat.

'No. Professor Rousseau sends her apologies. Her mother—'

'The Count will not be pleased.'

She had no comeback to that, other than to swing herself onto the withered and cracked upholstery of the passenger seat before he could drive away without her.

The Jeep lurched into life and she clutched her briefcase tighter in her lap as the vehicle tore up the narrow road. If you could call it a road, Grace thought, as it narrowed to little more than a one-lane track, zig-zagging up the cliff-face. She made the mistake of looking out of the car as he took another impossibly tight bend, and saw stones spraying over the edge of the cliff, spilling towards the boat now shrinking below. She squeezed her eyes shut.

'Do you think maybe you could drive a little slower?'

He shook his head gravely, muttered something under his breath.

'Only I would like to get to look at the discovery before I die.'

'The Count,' he almost grunted, ignoring her attempt at humour, 'he is expecting the Professor.'

'Yes, you said. I tried to explain—'

'He will not be pleased.'

Conversation was clearly not his forte. She tried to concentrate on the spectacular view across the expanse of Mediterranean to where the coastline of Italy was just visible in the distance, while trying not to think about the height of the cliff they were scaling that made such a magnificent view possible. But it was the subject of her driver's concern who stole her concentration and reminded her that the real reason for this coiling uneasiness in her gut was not down to anticipation at working on an ancient text, or motion sickness, or even the brooding castle, but dread.

Therese Rousseau had warned her. She'd said he was difficult and the driver's words did nothing to suggest the Professor had been unfair in her description. In fact, if anything, maybe she'd been a trifle flattering.

What exactly happened when the Count was not pleased? What was it that she had to look forward to?

At least the Jeep had managed to scale the cliff. The track was widening and now bordered in rocks she could tell had once been painted white, though now they were chipped and faded, their paint worn from exposure to the salt-laden air.

She shivered—the air was noticeably cooler at this height— and looked up in time to see the sun disappear behind the darkening clouds. And despite knowing in her brain that it meant nothing, that it was purely a meteorological phenomenon she was witnessing and not some kind of omen, even though she fought it with all she knew about the world, still she felt an unwanted and illogical sliver of fear slip down her spine.

The massive iron gates clanging shut behind them as they entered the castle grounds did nothing to assuage her unease. Now tension had her tightly wound, but she kept her breathing light as her driver crunched the gears while circling a tiered fountain featuring water nymphs and dolphins—a fountain that was as dry and neglected as the border of leggy, unkempt rosemary bushes that surrounded it.

Everywhere, it seemed, was shrouded in neglect, as if nothing had been touched for years.

And she wondered how anything as fragile as a book had survived in this place for the centuries it was reputed to have.

A miracle?

Or a curse?

This time the tremor seemed to chill her very bones. Great, she thought, doing her utmost to shake off the irrational sense

of impending danger. So much for priding herself on being
a logical scientist.

The Jeep jerked to a halt and the driver jumped out.
'Come,' he instructed, not bothering with her duffel this time,
but leaving it to her to retrieve as he pushed open giant tim-
ber doors that stretched at least twelve feet high and yet still
looked minuscule when compared to the mountainous castle
walls that dwarfed them.

And then they were inside and the temperature dropped
again. Her footsteps over the massive flagstones echoed in
the vast, empty entry hall. Or maybe that was just her heartbeat racing fast and loud…

For a thickset man, her guide moved fast, his short legs
carrying him surprisingly quickly up a flight of stairs that
looked as if they'd come straight from Sleeping Beauty's castle. 'Where are you taking me?' she asked from the bottom
of the stairs, but he gave no answer, and she didn't need it
to know there was no hope of him taking her directly to the
documents she'd come to examine.

The Count, she knew. The same Count who she'd been
warned repeatedly would not be pleased. She sighed and
started up the stairs behind him, lugging both her briefcase
and her duffel. Might as well get the unpleasantries over and
done with in that case. Maybe then she could get to work.

She followed him along a long passageway. The walls were
dressed with rich burgundy drapes, between which hung portraits of, she assumed, counts long gone. Superiority shone
from their steely eyes, along with a sense of entitlement for
the world and all its riches. The Counts of Volta, she sur-
mised, were not of modest, unassuming stock. But then why
should they be modest, with potent looks that were as masculinely beautiful as they were darkly dangerous?

Slight differences distinguished one from another—a slight
tilt of nose, an angle of jaw—and yet all of them in that long,
seemingly endless row bore the same dark eyes and brows,

topped by the same distinct hairline that intruded onto their temples in sharp points, almost like a shadow cast from... She stopped herself, refusing the link she'd made in her mind. They so did *not* resemble horns! She was being ridiculous even thinking it.

Besides, she'd researched the latest Count Volta late last night, after the Professor had called with her news, when both the excitement of the task ahead and the cryptic 'You'll be fine' had banished any thoughts of sleep. And she'd remembered then why his name had seemed vaguely familiar, remembered hearing around her eighteenth birthday news reports of the party boat explosion off the Costa Smerelda. Last night she'd read again of the shocking death toll and of the miracle survivor who'd lost his fiancée and his friends that night and who, scarred and bereft, had walked away and turned his back on both a promising career as a concert pianist and society.

The media had pursued him for a while, she'd read, seeking exclusives and exposés, before apparently tiring of the fruitless chase and moving on to juicier, more obliging celebrity prey. And so, entrenched in his self-imposed exile on his island home, he'd slipped into obscurity.

Who could blame him for cutting himself off from the world after an accident like that? Maybe it was no surprise he was 'difficult'. But it said something for the man that he hadn't kept the discovery of the documents secret. He would have known the potential for the discovery to once again focus the world's attention squarely on him. No wonder he'd insisted on only one specialist, and for the job to be completed inside a week.

Which was fine with her. She didn't want to hang around a crotchety old hermit and his crumbling castle a moment longer than necessary. She wouldn't get in his way and hopefully he'd stay out of hers.

Her guide came to an abrupt halt, rapping briefly on a pair of doors before poking his head inside one of them, leaving her no choice but to cool her heels behind him. 'She's here but it's not the Professor,' she heard him say. 'I've told the boat not to leave until you're ready.' And then he swept back past her without a glance, as if fleeing in case he was blamed for collecting the wrong baggage.

So that was why he hadn't brought her bag in and she'd had to lug it herself—because he thought she wasn't staying. If she'd needed anything to dispel any remaining shred of apprehension, her introduction as some kind of afterthought fitted the bill perfectly. She pushed open the door he'd left ajar.

'My name is Grace Hunter and I have a letter of introduction from Professor...' Her words shrivelled up in a throat suddenly drier than the fountain outside, and it might very well have been clogged with stranded sea nymphs and beached dolphins.

Where was the crotchety old hermit she'd been expecting? The modern-day Robinson Crusoe complete with beard and tattered clothes? Someone who matched the air of neglect that shrouded the rest of this barren island and its crumbling castle? But there was nothing tattered about the man who stood looking out of the window across the room from her now, nothing neglected.

'...Rousseau.'

The name fell heavily into the empty space between them. He stood still as a statue, his hands clasped behind his stiff back, clad in a suit tailored so superbly to his tall, lean body it almost looked part of him.

But it was his profile that captured her attention, and the clear similarities to his forebears lining the portrait gallery. His strong nose and resolute jaw, and the unmistakable mark of the Counts of Volta, the clearly defined dark hairline that intruded in sharp points at his temples. And he was every bit as powerfully beautiful as those who had gone before. Which made no sense at all...

She swallowed. 'Count Volta?'

CHAPTER THREE

Across the room she saw the flare of his nostrils. She heard his intake of air. She was even convinced she saw the grind of his jaw as he stared seemingly fixedly through the window. And then he turned, and the truth of his scars, the horror of his injuries, confronted her full-on.

A jagged line ripped down one side of his face from the corner of his eye through his jaw and down his neck, where it thankfully disappeared under the high collar of his jacket.

She gasped. She'd seen scars before. She'd witnessed the results of man's inhumanity to man during a year where youthful idealism had sent her to one of the world's hell-holes and spat her out at the end, cynical and dispirited. She'd thought she'd seen it all. And she'd seen worse. Much worse. And yet the sheer inequality of this man's scars—that one side of his face would be so utterly perfect and the other so tragically scored by scars—it seemed so wrong.

His eyes narrowed, glinting like water on marble. 'Didn't anyone ever tell you it's rude to stare?'

Chastened, she blinked and scrabbled for the pocket of her briefcase and the letter from the Professor she'd come armed with. 'Of course. Count Volta, Professor Rousseau apparently tried several times to contact you last night to tell you that she couldn't make it.' She pulled the envelope free and crossed the floor to hand it to him.

He looked down at the letter in her hand as if it was a poisoned chalice. 'You were not invited here.'

'Professor Rousseau's letter will, I'm sure, explain everything.'

'You are not welcome.' He turned back to the window, putting his back to her. 'Bruno will arrange for your immediate return to the mainland.'

His decision was so abrupt—so unjust!—that for a moment she felt the wind knocked out of her sails. He was dismissing her? Sending her away? Denying her the opportunity of working on the most important discovery since the Dead Sea Scrolls for no reason?

No way! 'I'm not going anywhere.' The words burst from her lips before she'd had a chance to think, a chance to stop them. 'I am here to do a job and I will not leave until it is done.'

He spun round and once again she was confronted with the two sides of him—each side of his face so different, each side compelling viewing, the masculinely perfect and the dreadfully scarred. Beauty and the beast, it occurred to her, co-existing under the one skin.

'Did you hear me? I said Bruno will arrange for your return.'

It was all she could do not to stamp her foot. 'And I said I'm not leaving!

One arm swept in a wide arc. 'I have no dealings with you. My arrangement was with Professor Rousseau.'

'No. According to the documents, your arrangement was with her business, Archival Survival. When the Professor was unable to come, she contracted me.'

He grunted, no way about to concede the point. 'So what is her excuse for being unable to fulfil her contractual obligations herself?'

'If you'd read this letter you'd know. Her mother is in hospital after suffering a major stroke and she's rushed to be with her while she clings to life. Admittedly, as excuses go, that's pretty thin. Clearly it's more about inconveniencing *you*.'

If his eyes were lasers, she figured, with the heated glare he gave her she'd be wearing holes right now, and she wondered if she'd overstepped the mark. She'd grown up in a family that prided itself on being straight-talking. Over the years she'd learned to curb that trait while in civilised company. The Count, she'd already decided, for all his flash clothes and a portrait gallery full of titled ancestors, didn't qualify.

'I expected an expert. I do not intend spending a week babysitting someone's apprentice.'

She sucked in air, hating the fact it was tinged with a hint of sandalwood and spice, with undertones of something else altogether more musky, hating the possibility that it might come from him, hating the possibility that there might be something about him she approved of when the rest of him was so damned objectionable.

But that was still okay, she figured, because finding something she might possibly like only made her more resentful towards him. 'Seeing you refuse to read this letter, where all the facts are set out in black and white, perhaps I should spell it out for you? I have a Masters in Fine Arts from Melbourne University and a PhD in Antiquities from Oxford, where my thesis was on the preservation and conservation of ancient texts and the challenge of discerning fraud where it was perpetrated centuries ago. So if there's an apprentice on this island right now, I don't think it's me. Does that make you feel more comfortable?'

He arched one critical eyebrow high. 'You look barely out of high school.'

'I'm twenty-eight years old. But don't take my word for it. Perhaps you'd like to check my passport?'

Dust motes danced on the slanted sunlit air between them, oblivious of the tension—dust motes that disappeared with those slanting rays as the sun was swallowed up by a cloud and the room darkened. She resisted the urge to shiver, resisted that damned illogical brain cell that suggested there was some connection between the Count's dark looks and the weather. And instead she decided that his momentary silence meant assent.

'And so right now I'd like to get to work. After all, I believe you want this text taken off your hands as soon as possible, and we've already wasted enough time, don't you agree? Perhaps you could arrange someone to show me to the documents so I might get started?'

He scowled as he took the letter from her hands then, scanning its contents, finding everything was as she said and finding nothing to arm him with the ammunition to demand she leave.

He wanted her gone.

He didn't want women around the place. Not young women, and definitely not halfway to pretty. He had his fix of women once a month, when the launch brought across a local village woman. He never asked her name; she never offered it. Each time she would just wait for him naked in the guest-suite bed, then throw back the covers and close her eyes…

And afterwards the launch would take her back to her village, considerably better off than before she had made the crossing.

No, Alessandro had no need for women.

He shrugged and tossed the letter down on his wide desk. What did it matter what the letter said or didn't say? 'I said you are not welcome here, Ms Hunter.'

She stiffened to stone right where she stood, her mouth pursing. '*Dr* Hunter, actually. And I will ensure my stay is as brief as possible. I have no desire to stay any longer than necessary where I am not welcome, I can assure you.'

He sniffed at the correction as he regarded her solemnly. She looked like a woman who had no desires, period. Sure, she was younger than the dried-up Professor, but with her scraped-back hair and that pursed mouth, and in khaki pants and T-shirt, it wasn't as if she was anything like the women who had once graced his arm and his bed.

God knew, another twenty years or so of staring into her desiccated papers and she'd probably be as dried up and crusty as the Professor. Maybe he had nothing to worry about.

And she was right about one thing: he did want the find off his hands as quickly as possible. If the Professor proved unable to do it personally because of her ailing mother someone else would have to be found, all of it spelling delay after delay.

He ground his teeth together. The longer he waited, the more likely news of the discovery would filter out. The last thing he wanted was the media sniffing around again, turning the place into some kind of fish tank.

'Then make your assessment as brief as possible and make us all happy by leaving.' He turned back to gaze out of the window again, knowing she would do exactly that. People always ran from him. And then he frowned, remembering the way her big blue eyes had stared at him...

Yes, she'd been shocked. But where was the revulsion? Where was the pity? Instead she'd examined him as one might regard some kind of science project.

And the snarling beast inside him didn't like that notion any better.

'I'd like to see the book now.'

He turned back, surprised she hadn't changed her mind and taken the opportunity to flee while his back was turned. She was surprisingly feisty, this one, holding her ground when many men twice her age and size would have gone running for the hills. Did she want the opportunity of examining and documenting this discovery so much that she had somehow summoned the will to fight for it? Or was she always this feisty?

Her eyes held his, bright and blue and cold as ice. Once women had looked at him with lust and desire. But that was long ago. There was no lust in Ms Hunter's eyes, no desire— or at least not for him. But there was something else he read in them. The yearning to become famous? Probably. This discovery, if it proved authentic, would probably make a young conservator's career.

'It's not all it's cracked up to be,' he said.

She blinked—a fan of black lashes against her peaches and cream complexion. And it occurred to him that it was almost a shame to condemn such translucent skin to the Professor's wrinkled fate. 'Pardon?'

A rap on the door and the reappearance of Bruno curtailed any response. 'The boat wishes to leave,' he grunted. 'Are you finished with the girl?'

And with the question came Alessandro's first smile of the day. In one way he was—though not the way his valet was clearly expecting. He'd agreed she could stay, and this meeting was now over. He'd planned to have Bruno take her to the book. He'd need to have little more to do with her. But *was* he finished with her?

Maybe not.

What would it take to make her run? What would it take to shake up those frosty blue eyes and strip off that sterile scientific cladding she wrapped herself so tightly in and see what really lay beneath? Besides, if he admitted the truth, he could do with a little entertainment. The woman might provide some mild amusement. She was only here for a few days. What possible harm could it do?

'No, I'm not finished with our charming guest, Bruno.' And this time he directed his words at her. 'In fact, I do believe I've scarcely begun. Come, *Dr* Hunter, and I'll show you to your precious documents.'

* * *

She left her luggage and briefcase where he directed, following him through a tangle of passageways, down wooden stairs that shifted and creaked under their footfall, and then down again—stone steps this time, that were worn into hollows by the feet of generations gone before—until she was sure they must be well below ground level, and the walls were lined with rock. And finally he stopped before a door that seemed carved from the stone itself.

He tugged on an iron ring set into the stone. 'Are you scared of the dark, Dr Hunter?' he asked over his shoulder, and she got the distinct impression he would love it if she were.

'No. That's never been a particular phobia of mine.'

'How fortunate,' he said, sounding as if he thought it was anything but. Then the door shifted open and she got a hint of what was to come—a low, dark passageway that sloped down through the rock. When he turned to her the crooked smile she'd seen in his office was back. 'Every castle should have at least one secret tunnel, don't you think?'

'I would have to say it's practically *de rigueur*, Count Volta.'

His smile slipped a little, she noted with satisfaction, almost as if she hadn't answered the way he'd expected. Tough. The fact was she *was* here, and with any luck she was on her way to the missing pages of the *Salus Totus*. Although what they were doing all the way down here...

A slow drip came from somewhere around her, echoing in the space, and while she wished she'd at least grabbed a jacket before descending into the stone world beneath the castle, it was the book she was more worried about now.

'You are taking me to the book?'

'Of course.'

'But what is it doing down here?'

'It was found down here.'

'And you left it here?'

His regarded her coldly, as if surprised she would question his decision. 'The caves have guarded their treasure for centuries. Why would I move it and risk damaging such a potentially precious thing?'

Plenty of reasons, she thought. Like the drip that echoed around the chamber, speaking of moisture that could ruin ancient texts with mould and damp. Something so ancient, even if it proved to be a forgery, should be kept where the temperature and humidity could be regulated and it would be safe from things that scuttled and foraged in the night. She didn't expect the Count to necessarily know that, but she would have expected him to have had the sense to move the find somewhere safe.

Inside the chamber there was just enough light to see with the door open. She blinked, waiting for her eyes to adjust, but then he pulled the door closed behind them with a crunch and the light was swallowed up in inky blackness and there was nothing for her eyes to adjust to.

Afraid of the dark? No, she wasn't, but neither did she like being holed up in it. Not with him. She could hear his breathing, she could damn well smell that evocative masculine scent of his, and she dared not move for fear she might brush against him in the dark. She heard the scratch of something rough, caught a hint of phosphorus and saw a spark that burst into flame atop a torch he held. The shifting yellow light threw crazy shadows against the walls, illuminating a cable running overhead with light bulbs hanging sporadically.

'You couldn't have just turned on the lights, I suppose?'

'A storm last night knocked out the cable from the mainland, which is no doubt why your Professor could not contact me. Power is back on in the castle, but the caves will take longer. Don't you like the torchlight, Ms Hunter. I find it so much more—*atmospheric*.'

He had just enough accent to curl around the word, trans-

forming it in a way that turned it somehow darkly sensual—
something that put a peculiar shiver down her spine. Peculiar,
because instead of the chill she'd expected it warmed her
in places she didn't like to think about. Not around him.
Shadows danced on the walls of the tunnel, light flickered
against the unscarred side of his face, highlighting cheekbone
and forehead and that sharply defined hairline, throwing his
eyes into a band of black from which only a glint of amusement escaped.

And she could tell he was laughing at her.

Damn him.

'It's fine, I guess, if you're interested in atmosphere. Right
now I'm more interested in getting a look at those pages.'

He gave a mock bow in the shadowed darkness. 'As you
command,' he said, and led the way down the tunnel. Deeper
and deeper through the winding channel through the rock
they walked, footsteps echoing on the dusty floor, the yellow
flame of the torch flickering in the cool air, lighting the way,
but never far enough to see more than a few feet at a time.
They passed other tunnels that dived away, left and right,
and she wondered how you would ever find your way out if
the light went out and you were alone down here. She paused
to look over her shoulder at one such intersection, trying to
get a glimpse of the path behind, but the darkness had swallowed up the view, along with her sense of direction, and she
realised that she'd never find her way out alone.

Great. So she had no choice but to trust a man who didn't
want her here and seemed to delight in making her uncomfortable—a man who was leading her through a maze of tunnels a Minotaur would be happy to call home with nothing
but a lighted torch to find their way.

Bad call. Did she really want to think about Minotaurs and
labyrinths now, when she was down here with a man whose
broad shoulders filled the width of the tunnel? Especially
when she thought about what had happened to the seven

youths and seven maidens from Athens who'd been thrown into the labyrinth to their doom as a tribute to the Minoan king.

Maybe she should have brought a ball of string...

Something clapped down hard on her shoulder—his hand—and she panicked, every instinct telling her to flee. It was only its weight that kept her anchored to the ground.

'You don't want to get lost in here,' whispered a deep voice in her ear, his breath fanning her hair, warm in the cool tunnel air. 'We might never find you again.'

She turned slowly, hoping to calm her face and her rapid breathing before he could see just how much he'd frightened her, but she was fighting a losing battle on slowing her heart-rate, given what his proximity was doing to her nervous system and his scent was doing to her defences. 'You startled me,' she admitted, licking her lips as she looked up at him in the torchlight, struck again by the difference between one side of his face and the other—one side all strong, masculine lines and sharply defined places, the other so monstrously scarred.

His left eye had thankfully escaped the worst, she was close enough to see, and his strong nose and wide mouth were blessedly untouched. It was as if the skin of his cheek and neck had been torn apart and rejoined in a thick, jagged line that snaked up his throat and cheek and tapered to the corner of one eye.

Both those dark eyes narrowed as they looked down at her now. 'Come,' he said gruffly, dropping his hand from her shoulder and turning away.

Her shoulder felt inexplicably bereft—*cold*—the warmth from his long fingers replaced with a bone-deep chill, and she hugged her shoulders as she trailed behind him through the maze of tunnels, trying not to think of the weight of rock above their heads. The tunnels had clearly been here for a long time—surely the ceiling could hold just a little longer? Especially when they must be getting close to their goal.

A surge of adrenaline washed through her. Could the pages truly be from the lost copy of the *Salus Totus*? How complete would they be? Could she really be close to solving the mystery of generations? The mystery of the contents of those lost pages?

'Watch your step,' he said, then asked her to wait as he descended a short steep flight of stairs cut into the rock. At the bottom he turned, holding the torch above him so she could see her way down the narrow steps, but it was the hand he offered to her that looked the more threatening. A large hand, she noted. Tapered fingers. Would it be churlish to refuse? But there was nothing to be afraid of—she'd survived the last time he'd touched her, hadn't she?

And so she slipped her hand into his, felt his long fingers wrap around her own, and tried not to think too much about how warm they felt against her skin. How strong his grip. How secure.

'Thank you,' she said, lifting her eyes to his as she negotiated the last step, wondering at the suddenness with which he turned his face away, only to be distracted by the sudden space around them here, as the tunnel widened into a wide, low room. There were tables set around, and shelves built into the walls containing racks of bottles—dozens and dozens of bottles. 'What is this place?' she asked, stepping around him.

'Welcome to my wine cellar. Here you'll find every vintage of Vino de Volta going back to 1797.'

'Hell of a place for a wine cellar,' she mused, strolling past the racks of bottles, pausing to peer at a label here and there, the lover of ancient and even not-so-ancient treasures inside her completely fascinated.

'There's more,' he said, 'through here.' He dipped his head under a low doorway leading to another room, this one more like a cavern, its walls similarly stacked.

She followed him in, made a wide circle as she took it all in. It was the perfect place for a wine cellar, the air cool and dry, with no telltale dripping. And a spark of excitement flashed through her. Because if it was the perfect place to store wine...

'Are they here?' she asked, unable to keep the excitement from her voice. 'Is this where the pages were found?'

Her enthusiasm lit up the cavern more effectively than any amount of torchlight. She was like a child, excited about a present she'd asked Santa for and for which she'd promised to be good, her eyes bright with expectation, a dancing flame alive on their surfaces.

And he felt a sudden twist in his gut that made him wheel away, for she was so vibrant and alive and everything that Adele had once been—everything that he no longer was.

Blackness surged up and threatened to swallow him whole; not the black of the caves but the blackness that came from within, the blackness that had been his constant companion since that night. He'd thought he'd learned to control it, but it was there, lurking in the scars that lined his face and body, lurking on the very edges of his sanity, waiting to seize control, and he cursed himself for giving in to the urge to amuse himself with her. Cursed himself for putting a hand to her slim shoulder. Cursed himself for wanting more and for then finding an excuse to take her fragile hand in his own.

It had been a long time since he'd touched a woman he hadn't had to pay.

Such a long time...

He dragged in one breath and then another, forcing the blackness back down, refusing to give in to its power, determined not to succumb. Not here. Not now. 'This way,' he managed to grind out, through a jaw that ached with the effort of those two simple words.

Behind him she blinked, letting go a breath she hadn't realised she'd been holding. What had just happened? For a while she'd imagined he was loosening up a bit around the edges, losing some of his antagonism and resentment towards her. She'd even sensed he was getting some kind of sick pleasure from his teasing about secret passageways and the atmospherics of torchlight.

And then suddenly he'd changed. In the blink of an eye his entire body had set rigid, his skin pulling tight over a face in which his eyes had turned harder than the stone walls that enclosed them. As he'd turned from her she'd witnessed the tortured expression that strained his features and in the shadow-laden light had turned the scarred side of his face into the mask of a monster. A legend, she told herself, her heart thumping as she was reminded again of the story of the Minotaur. *Just a legend.*

But she must have gasped, she must have made some small sound, for he turned back, studying her face, his eyes strangely satisfied with what he saw as he leaned closer to her. 'What's wrong, Dr Hunter? Do I frighten you at last?'

'No,' she said shakily, praying for composure, trying to block out thoughts of monsters and Minotaurs and the twisted maze of passageways that lay between her and freedom, wondering if he would chase her if she ran. *Wondering what he might do if do if he caught her.* 'No.' This time she said it with more certainty, even though her heart was still pumping furiously and her breathing too shallow. Once again she sought to regain control. 'I'm not afraid of you, Count Volta.'

He drew back momentarily on an intake of air, his lips curling to bare his teeth, before he exhaled in a rush as he came closer again. 'Then you should be, Dr Hunter. You should be.'

He was too close. She could feel the heat from his face and his breath against her skin. But, while her heart was thumping loudly, she realised it wasn't fear that was making her blood pound and her heart race.

It was the man himself.

And in spite of herself, in spite of his implicit threat, she felt herself drawn towards him, her skin prickling with aware-ness, her breasts strangely, *achingly* full.

And from somewhere deep inside her, some dark, danger-ous place she hadn't known existed, she managed to summon a smile. 'If you want to frighten me, you'll have to do better than that.'

The torchlight flickered gold in his dark eyes, until she could almost imagine it dancing with the devil within—the devil that made him grind his teeth together as if he was bat-tling with himself even as he leaned still closer. So close that his face was scant millimetres from hers. So close that his lips were a mere breath away…

CHAPTER FOUR

SHE heard his growl of frustration as he swung away, leaving her with only heated air scented by his musky scent and wondering shakily why she was trying to bait him, what she was trying to achieve. What was happening to her?

'Do you want to see these papers or not?' he said, already heading deeper into the secret cellar, and she thanked her lucky stars that one of them was thinking straight. For what had she been thinking? That he was going to kiss her? A man she'd met barely an hour ago? A man who had made it plain she was not welcome here, who had objected to her presence and then set out to make her uncomfortable in his?

Difficult? The description didn't come close. The sooner she was finished with her assessment and away from the Isola de Volta, and its scarred Count, the better.

Tentatively she followed him into a smaller cavern, the doorway rammed firm with beams the size of tree trunks. The room was sparsely furnished, with an old table and two chairs. There was a well-thumbed pack of cards in one corner, and what looked like a bunch of old ledgers on a shelf nearby.

'Over there,' he said, indicating towards the shelf. 'Do you see it?'

Her hopes took a dive. Surely she hadn't been brought all the way out here—surely she wasn't being subjected to all this—for a bunch of mouldy old records? But then to one side she saw something else—what looked like some kind of cleft in the rock-face, almost invisible except for the shadow cast by the torch he'd shoved into a ring set into the wall. Intrigued, she took a step closer. Could that be what he meant?

He was already there—impatient to be rid of her, she guessed—his hand seemingly disappearing into the rock-face before it re-emerged, this time holding a flat parcel.

In the flicker and spit of torchlight she held her breath, excitement fizzing in her veins as he brought the package to the table, depositing it more gently there than she could imagine someone his size doing anything. And then he stood abruptly. 'This is what you want so desperately to see?'

He was angry with her, but right now his bad mood rolled off her. Her eyes, her senses, her full attention were all focused on the parcel on the table. She licked her lips, her mouth dry with anticipation, her eyes assessing. A quick estimation told her the size was about right for something containing the long-lost pages, but that didn't mean this was it.

She took a step closer, and then another, the man beside the table and his disturbing presence all but forgotten now as her eyes drank in the details of the worn pouch that looked as if it was made from some kind of animal skin, of the rough clasp that had been fashioned to keep the parcel together. A pin of ivory, she guessed, stained yellow by the passage of time.

'May I?' she said, with no more than a glance in his direction, unwilling to take her eyes from this precious discovery for more than a second lest it disappear in a puff of smoke. She should wait until they'd brought the package back to the castle and she had the right lighting and the right conditions. She should wait until she had her tools by her side.

She should wait.

Except that she couldn't.

Adrenaline coursed through her. She had to look. She had to see. So she slipped her arms from her backpack and pulled a new pair of gloves from the pocket where she kept them and drew them on, fingers almost shaking with excitement. *Calm down.* She heard the Professor's voice in her head, heeded it, and willed herself to slow down. To breathe.

She knew what she was looking for. She'd studied what little remained of the *Salus Totus*. She knew the language and the artwork. She knew what inks the artists had used and how they'd been sourced, and she knew what animal's skin had gone to make the parchment. And nothing on this earth— *nothing*—was more important to her than the thrill of seeing what could be those missing pages and seeing them *now*.

With gloved hands she gently prised the clasp open and pulled back the leather wrapping, folded like an envelope around the treasure within.

A blank page met her hungry eyes, but the bubble of disappointment was happily pricked in the knowledge that, whatever their purpose, whoever had taken these pages had realised they needed some form of protection.

She took a steadying breath. A big one. Gingerly, she lifted the cover sheet and moved it to one side.

And what little breath she had left was knocked clear out of her lungs.

Colour leapt from the page—vivid reds, intense blues, yellows that ranged from freshly picked corn to burnished gold. And even in the flicker of torchlight the quill strokes of another age stood out clear and bold, the Latin text as fresh as the day it had been written, although it was clear the parchment itself was old, despite being in amazing condition.

Her eyes drank in the details. The similarities to the remnants of the *Salus Totus* were unmistakable. And tears sprang to her eyes. Whether authentic or a cleverly crafted fraud, it was a thing of beauty.

'Well? Do you think it's what you're looking for?'

She jumped and swiped at her eyes, suddenly embarrassed

at the unexpected display of emotion. She'd been so absorbed she'd forgotten completely there was anyone else present.

And the last thing she wanted was for this man to see her shed tears. So she turned away and delved through her backpack again, pulling out one of the acid-free boxes she'd packed, thankful for the excuse to have something to do so that she didn't have to look at him.

'I don't know. I have to get it back to the castle. Do you have somewhere I can use as a study?' Reluctantly she replaced the protective cover over the page and refolded the bundle before slipping it into the slim box. She had to get it back before she was tempted to look at the next page, and then the next. She could prove nothing down here but her insatiable curiosity.

When finally she did look up, wondering why he hadn't responded, his features looked strained, a flicker of inner torment paining his eyes. But then he merely nodded and said through gritted teeth, 'I'll take you there now.'

He said nothing as he led the way back to the castle along the twisted passages and for that she was grateful. Her blood was alive and sparking with possibilities. Her mind was already processing the little she'd seen and working through the steps she'd take once she got the package back somewhere with decent lighting and her tools.

And as for her other senses? They seemed one hundred percent preoccupied with the Count. That damned evocative scent teased her at every turn, the fluid movement of his limbs was like a magnet for her eyes, and then there was his shadow, looming menacingly against the wall…

She swallowed. He was so big he dwarfed her. He was powerful and dangerous and he was angry, and he'd made it clear he didn't want her here. He should frighten her. That would make sense. But instead she felt something no less primal and every bit more confusing.

Because he excited her on a level so deep she'd never

known it existed. He caused a quickening of her heart and an ache in her breasts and made her wonder what he'd have tasted like if he'd kissed her back there…

Madness, she decided. He'd done the right thing in turning away. She didn't want to kiss him. She was here to do a job. She didn't need the complications.

Yet still she wondered…

Soon they were back in the castle, past the stone door and making their way up the winding stairs. There was space here, and light, though gloomy and thin. The sound of the wind was growing louder. She wondered if things might be different now they were above ground, not so strained and tense between them. And then a shutter banged somewhere and curtains fluttered on unseen draughts.

'A storm is building,' he told her over his shoulder. Unnecessarily, she thought. Given the setting and her dark companion, she would have been more surprised if a storm *wasn't* building.

Then he did surprise her, by showing her into the room that was to be her office. It was remarkably well thought out. No external windows to let in draughts or damp. A large desk to spread her things out with lamps for extra lighting. A heater in one corner. A dehumidifier in another. She circled the room, stopped before the desk and nodded her appreciation as she took it all in.

'Did the Professor give you a shopping list?'

She turned and took a step back and gasped, so surprised to find him within a metre of her that she took another involuntary step backwards against the desk, one hand reaching down to steady her, the other over her pounding heart, willing it to slow. So much for his impact being less intense above the ground. An aura surrounded him, a mantle of power and presence, and a scent that wove its way into her senses like a drug. So how exactly was she supposed to calm her racing heart?

His eyes glinted, his lips curving into the slightest smile, as if he was relishing her reaction. 'You really think I would take chances with something potentially so precious?' He nodded knowingly before she could reply. 'But of course, you do. You thought I was irresponsible to leave it in the caves, didn't you? In the place that had harboured it safely for perhaps hundreds of years.'

She licked her lips, regretting the gesture immediately when his scent turned to taste on her lips. Regretting it more when she saw his eyes follow the sweep of her tongue.

'I'll admit it,' she said, trying to get a foothold on the conversation and justify her position. Because she *had* thought exactly that. Until she'd felt the air down there and realised it was probably the reason why the pages were in such good condition. 'It did seem a trifle reckless, at least—'

'Reckless?' he repeated, jumping on the word, his eyes gleaming, refusing to let hers go. 'I take it you're not a fan of being reckless, Ms Hunter?'

'No, but—'

'But you make exceptions?'

'No! That wasn't what I was going to say at all.'

His eyes gleamed, searching hers with a heated intensity that left her breathless, until with a blink they cooled and flicked towards his wristwatch and then at the door, as if he had somewhere he had to be. 'No. You really don't seem the type. And now I shall leave you. Anything else you need, Bruno will see to it for you.'

Right now she could uncharacteristically do with a stiff drink, though she'd quite happily settle for tea. She was still strangely stinging from that 'you really don't seem the type', and she wasn't even sure why. She'd never been reckless in her entire life. She'd been too driven, so focused on what she wanted that even her friends at university had affectionately labelled her a nerd.

'How will I find Bruno?' she asked, surprising herself with

how calm she sounded now that he'd eased away and given her space. 'If I need him?'

'Bruno will find you. He has a way of anticipating one's needs.'

A psychic henchman? But of course a count would need one of those, along with his secret tunnels and his crumbling castle. It was just what she needed to improve her mood. 'Excellent,' she rejoined, with exaggerated enthusiasm and a smile designed to get right under his skin. 'Then it appears I'm all set. I'd better get to work.'

And with a glower and a nod he was gone and she could breathe again.

She slumped into the nearest chair. The pages, she thought, her fingers pressed to her temples. Think about the pages and all they mean to you. And she would, she promised herself, just as soon as she'd caught her breath. Being with the Count was like being caught in a whirlwind and spun in circles until she was spat out again, dizzy and confused.

Difficult? The man was turning out to be her worst nightmare.

A sharp rap on the door and she jumped, instantly alert, but it was only Bruno, bearing a tray.

'Something to eat,' he grunted, placing the tray on a side table.

Grace blinked and caught a whiff of something warm and savoury. Frittata, she realised as she approached, feeling suddenly hungry and remembering she hadn't eaten for hours. And, if she was not mistaken, a pot of tea. She lifted the lid and took a sniff. English breakfast. Maybe he really was psychic. 'How did you know I'd prefer tea to coffee?'

He shrugged. 'You're *inglese*, no?'

'Australian,' she corrected. And he shrugged again, as if it were the same thing, and disappeared.

Lucky guess, she figured, and poured herself a cup, enthusiasm once again building inside her. A quick meal and she could get to work. Strange, though, given how excited she'd been at getting this opportunity, that something could distract her to such an extent that at times she almost forgot the book completely.

Well, not something—*someone*. And maybe he was difficult and dangerous and tortured and gave her heated glances that made her squirm—still, it wasn't like her at all.

He paced his office, walking past windows rattling with the wind and splattered with raindrops from the first of the coming squalls. Clouds obliterated what was left of the sun until day turned almost to night.

He paced the room uncaring. He saw nothing but the expression on her face when she'd turned that cursed page. It had been bad enough when she'd thought they were close. She'd looked so alive with hope and anticipation. He hadn't thought it could get any worse, that she could look any more alive than she had in that moment.

And then she'd turned that cover page and her eyes had widened, her face had lit up and her whole body had damned near ignited.

He'd damned near combusted watching her. He'd been rock-hard with need and so hot it was a wonder he hadn't turned to a column of ash right there and then. And all he'd been able to wonder since then was if that was the way she looked when she was looking at some piece of ancient parchment, how good might she look when she came apart in his arms?

He wanted to find out.

He burned to find out.

What was wrong with him? She was a scientist, with scraped-back hair and a passion for ancient relics, and he was lusting after her? Damn! What on earth had possessed him to let her stay?

Alessandro threw himself into his chair and then spun straight out of it, reaching for his phone. God, he didn't need this!

Bruno answered on the second ring.

'Fetch the woman from the village,' he growled.

There was hesitation at the end of the phone and he could almost hear Bruno's mind working out that it was not quite a month since her last visit. But instead he said, 'The boat will not come with the storm brewing.'

'Offer them double,' he ordered, and hung up.

Five minutes later Bruno called back. 'The captain says it's too rough. He will bring her tomorrow.'

'I don't want her tomorrow!' This time he slammed the phone down, turning his gaze out through the windows to where the waves were wearing white caps from which the wind whipped spray metres into the air. And then rain lashed the windows until they were running like a river and the sea beyond blurred to grey.

Curse the damned weather! How dared it confound him when he needed a woman?

But there was already a woman on the island.

He wheeled away, trying hard to lose that thought. He could see her even now, poring over her precious pages as if they were the Holy Grail. In that moment he'd seen inside her. He'd seen beyond the scientist who made out she had no desires. He'd seen the woman beneath—a woman born for passion.

And she was waiting for you to kiss her.

He strode down the passageway, raking hands through his hair, not knowing where he was going, refusing to give credence to the sly voice in his head that refused to shut up.

She baited you.

She didn't know what she was asking.

She wants you.

No. No. And *no*! She did not want him. She was a fool. She had no idea.

But you want her...

He found himself outside her room, the sliver of light under the door telling him she was still working, his hands clenching and unclenching at his sides.

Would she welcome his visit?

Would she welcome being spread over that wide desk, scattering her precious papers, while he buried himself in her depths? Would her eyes light up for him the way they had in the cave? Would her entire body shimmer with desire and explode with light?

Blood pounded in his ears. His fingers were on the doorknob.

Or would she close her eyes and turn away?

He could not bear it if she turned away...

Blackness, thick and viscous, oozed up from the depths. His fingers screwed into a ball as he forced it down.

Maybe she wouldn't. Maybe she was different. She didn't shy away from him. She didn't recoil in horror. She treated him as if he was almost normal—as if his scars didn't exist.

But you're not normal, the dark voices said. *You can never be normal again.*

The blackness welled up like a rolling wave. What had he been thinking? Why was he doing this to himself?

He should have made her leave when he'd had the chance!

He pushed away from the door, forced his feet to walk, but he'd gone no more than a few paces when he heard the door open behind him.

'Count Volta?'

He dragged in air, turned and nodded stiffly. 'Dr Hunter.'

She had a hand on her chest, as if she'd been frightened of who or what she might find in the passageway. 'I was just about to go to bed. I thought I heard a noise. Did you want something?'

God, yes.

'No. I'm sorry if I disturbed you.' He didn't want to think about Dr Hunter and bed. And then, because he should be interested, 'How does your investigation progress?'

Her eyes lit up that way they did until he would swear they almost shimmered with excitement. 'The pages are wonderful. Do you want to have a look before I put them away?'

On that same desk, when all he wanted was to spread her limbs and plunge into her slick depths and feel her incandescent exhilaration explode around him?

'No!' he said, so forcefully that she took a small step backwards and he had to suck in air to regain his composure. 'Maybe tomorrow,' he added more gently. 'It's getting late. Goodnight, Dr Hunter. Sleep well.'

He wouldn't sleep, he knew, as he descended the wide stairs leading to the ground floor. Not now, not after seeing her again. Instead he would read in the library and listen to the storm continue to build outside. He would take comfort in the savagery of the elements and the pounding violence of the sea. He would be at one with its endless torment.

And perhaps in the morning he might have Bruno fetch the woman from the village after all. God knew, books weren't going to cut it tonight. He would need something.

In the gloom of light he passed the doorway to the ballroom, a flash of lightning illuminating the empty space. Empty but for the grand piano sitting bereft in the far corner of the room.

He paused and gazed at the imprint the lightning had left behind and felt a pang for something long gone. Across the marble tiles, under the rumble of thunder, he approached the instrument like a one-time friend whose friendship had been soured by time. Cautiously. Mistrustfully.

Once he'd known her intimately. Known her highs and her lows and how to wring every piece of emotion from her.

She'd been a thing of beauty when the world had been all about beauty.

Before life had soured and turned ugly.

Yet still she sat there, black and sleek, totally shameless. And even now she beckoned, luring him like the memories of a mistress he hadn't quite finished with before they'd parted company.

And what surprised him more than anything was that he was tempted. He lifted the lid, ran his fingers along the keys, hit a solitary note that rang out in the empty ballroom and felt something twist inside him.

He could have put the lid down then. He could have walked away. But the way his fingers rested on the keys, familiar yet foreign, wouldn't let him go. Outside the waves crashed; the thunder boomed until the windows rattled. Inside his fingers reacquainted themselves with the cool ivory. He let them find their own way. He let them remember. Let them give voice to his damaged heart.

She woke with a start, her breath coming fast, her heart thumping, not knowing what had woken her, just grateful to escape from her dreams. She reached over to snap on her bedside light but the switch just clicked uselessly from side to side. Great. The storm must have taken out the power again.

The wind howled past the windows, searching for a way in. The sea boomed below, the waves pounding at the very foundations of the island.

What had woken her? Maybe it had been nothing. Certainly nothing she could do anything about now. She settled back down, willing her breathing to calm, not sure if she wanted to head straight back into the heated confusion of her dreams. She ran her hands thought her hair. No way did she want to go back there.

Often when she was working on a piece she would dream of her work, her mind busy even in sleep, imagining the artists and scribes who had produced whatever artefact she was studying. Often her mind would work at solving the puzzles of who and what and why, even when those answers had been lost in time.

But not tonight. Tonight her dreams had been full of one man. A scarred count. Menacing and intense. Unwelcoming to the point of rudeness and beyond, and yet at the same time strangely magnetic. Strangely compelling.

He'd been watching her in her dream, she remembered with a shudder. Not just looking at her—she knew the difference—but *watching* her, his black-as-night eyes wild and filled with dark desires and untold heat. And even now she could remember the feel of that penetrating gaze caress her skin like the sizzling touch of a lover's hand. Even now her skin goose-bumped and her breasts firmed and her nipples strained to peaks.

She shook her head, trying to clear the pictures from her mind; she punched her pillow as if that was the culprit, putting them there when she knew it probably had more to do with the storm. The lightning and thunder were messing with her brainwaves, she told herself. All that electrical energy was messing with the connections in her mind. It was madness to consider any other option. Madness.

She didn't even like the man!

She was just snuggling back down into the pillow-soft comfort of her bed, determined to think about the pages and the translations she would commence, when she heard it— what sounded like a solitary note ringing out into the night. But the sound was whisked away by the howling wind before she could get make sense of it.

She'd almost forgotten about it when there came another, hanging mournful and lonely in the cold night air. She blinked in the inky darkness, her ears straining for sounds that had no place in the storm.

And then, in a brief lull in the wind, she heard what

sounded like a chord this time, an achingly beautiful series of notes that seemed to echo the pain of the raging storm. Curious, she stretched out one hand, reaching for her watch, groping for the button to illuminate the display and groaning when she saw what time it was. Three-forty-five.

She had to be imagining things. Lightning flashed outside, turning her room to bright daylight for a moment before it plunged back into darkness. A boom of thunder followed, shaking the floor and windows and sending a burst of rain pelting against the windows.

She pulled back her arm and buried herself deeper under the thick eiderdown. She had to be dreaming. That or she really was going mad.

CHAPTER FIVE

Morning brought surprisingly clear skies with little trace of the storm that had threatened to rend the night apart. Grace blinked as she drew open the curtains and gazed out over the view. Every surface sparkled with its recent wash, the sapphire sea calm now but for a breeze playfully tickling at its surface. Not a cloud in the sky as far as she could see. She looked up and promptly revised her weather report. Not a cloud in the sky—except for the wispy white one hovering over the castle. She smiled, feeling brighter despite the nighttime's interruptions. Like the tunnels underneath the castle, it would almost be disappointing if the cloud weren't there.

She wasn't left to wonder about the arrangements for breakfast. True to the Count's prediction, Grace had no sooner bathed and dressed than Bruno appeared with a breakfast tray. She didn't mind if she was being snubbed by being made to take her meals alone; the arrangement suited her. Less chance of running into anyone, she figured. At least less chance of running into the Count. She wasn't sure she was ready for another encounter so soon after last night's discomfiting dreams.

And even though she had some questions about the pages, like how he thought they might have come to be in the caves below the castle and who might have left them there, they could wait until he came looking for her. He was sure to come and check how long she thought she would be here.

She was back in her makeshift office across the hall before eight. She'd photographed each of the pages yesterday, taking her time to get detailed photographs of every page and then more detailed shots of the cut edges where they'd been sliced from the book.

The rest of the day she'd spent making meticulous notes on the condition of each of the pages. For something reputed to be upwards of six hundred years old, they were remarkably well preserved, a fact that at first had her doubting they could possibly be authentic and wondering if they were nothing more than a clever forgery. After all, nobody really knew what had been in the missing pages, only that the book and its prayers had been famous for their healing words.

And yet the more she'd examined the pages, the more she'd been convinced they were the genuine article. It couldn't be confirmed until samples were matched with what little remained of the *Salus Totus*, but she almost didn't need that confirmation right now to be sure. And the longer she examined the pages, the more certain she was that this had the potential to be the very biggest discovery of the twenty-first century.

And she was at the heart of it.

Her heart raced with the potential. People worked thankless long decades in this industry, re-examining texts already long known, searching for an angle, a point of difference with which to elevate their careers out of obscurity. Seldom did people have an opportunity like this, the chance to examine a new discovery practically thrust upon them.

It was really happening.

And now, because the pages were in such amazingly good condition and she didn't have to spend time stabilising what was left, she could get to work on the translation. Some time this morning the power had been restored and gratefully she snapped on the lamps she'd arranged around the desk.

She'd recognised just an odd word or two as she'd performed yesterday's tasks and it had been tempting to stop and decipher more. Now she had the luxury of time to study them more closely. So it was with a heart bursting with possibilities that she retrieved the package from the box in which she'd stored it and gently placed the first page in front of her.

It was hours later before she happened to glance at her watch. Excited about her work so far, she knew she had to move, so she stood and did a few stretches before heading to her room across the hall and the jug of water she had left there.

She poured herself a glass and took a long drink, gazing out of the window, musing over the pages, before her eyes caught on a movement below the castle. A boat was nearing the dock—it looked like the same boat that had brought her over yesterday, although she'd got the impression from the way the men spoke that the provisions runs happened no more than once or twice a week. She glanced down and saw Bruno standing ready to meet it. Curious, she waited for it to dock, wondering what they were bringing this time.

Make that who, she amended, as a raven-haired woman was handed by a smiling skipper to the shore. A striking woman too, in a peasant top and skirt that showed off a tiny waist and generous curves. With a laugh and a wave to the skipper, she pulled a scarf around her shoulders and climbed into the Jeep alongside Bruno. Grace lost sight of them as they started up the cliff track.

Who was she? Grace had got the impression visitors weren't exactly welcome here. She shrugged and drained the rest of the glass. Maybe someone who worked at the castle. And with any luck a cook, given how hungry she suddenly felt.

Barely ten minutes later she was back at work when Bruno appeared, a very welcome tray in his hands. Whatever was on it, it smelled wonderful. She smiled and thanked him as he put it down on a table set a safe distance away from the desk and her work, even though she knew her words wouldn't make a dent in his grizzled visage.

'You're busy today,' she said. He merely grunted in response, peering at her from under tangled brows that looked like something that had been washed up in a storm. 'I saw you down at the dock. Who's the woman? Does she work here?'

He threw her a dark look. 'The woman is not your concern.'

'No, of course not. I just thought it might be nice to say hello—'

'Forget the woman!' he said, marching back to the door. 'She is not here for your benefit.'

The door closed behind him with a bang. Okay, maybe his message was none too subtle, but he was right. She should just get on with the job. At least then she could finish up here and leave. God knew, the prospect was tempting.

She was waiting for him. He let himself into the darkened room, the ache in his loins more insistent than ever after a night spent torturing himself thinking about that damned Dr Hunter. He refused to let himself think of her as anything else. He needed to think of her as a cold-blooded scientist and not as a woman.

Which made no sense when all he had wanted last night was have that woman bucking beneath him.

Why was she doing this to him? And how?

He dragged in air. Damn her. He was hard as a rock, his loins aching with need and another woman waiting naked in bed for him. Why was he even thinking about her?

He growled and approached the bed, shucking off his robe and tossing it to the floor, already half dizzy with the heady anticipation of release. His erection rocked free, heavy and hard. He steadied it with one hand to don protection and felt his searing, throbbing heat against his palm. *Dio*, he needed this.

He pulled back the covers and stared down at her in the

dim light. She was smiling knowingly, even though her eyes were dreamily closed, her head tipped back as if she was already in ecstasy, her hands busy at her breasts, tugging at her nipples, making them hard for him. Usually he'd spend some time with those breasts, but today his need was too great.

'Open your legs,' he commanded, and if she wondered at his brusque manner she didn't show it in the way she acquiesced without a murmur. And why shouldn't she do what he asked she when she was going home with the equivalent of a month's wages in her pocket? She'd do anything he asked and more.

He gazed down at her, took in the glossy hair splayed over the pillow, her olive skin with its satin-like sheen in the half-light, her breasts plump and peaked. He was rock-hard and wanting and he wondered why the hell he was hesitating and not already inside her.

Until he realised that there was somewhere else he'd rather be.

With a cry of frustration he snapped on the light. 'Get dressed,' he ordered. 'Bruno will take you to the boat.'

'Did I do something wro—?'

He was reaching for his robe and tugging it on, but not before she'd opened her eyes to plead, no doubt worried she would not be paid. He caught the exact moment of change, when her eyes moved from protest to revulsion, and she pulled the covers back over herself as if to protect herself from his hideousness.

With a roar he ripped the covers straight back off. 'Just go!'

He could wallow in them if he wanted. He could let those black waves rise up and swallow him whole, sucking him back to that dark time and those dark nights when there was no respite, no relief.

Or he could deal with the problem, get rid of the source

of his aggravation, and be able to breathe in his own space again.

He would not be sucked back.

He would deal with the problem.

Because everything had been fine until *she* had come along. She would just have to leave.

Now.

He headed to her office to tell her exactly that. After all, it wasn't as if the pages were in terrible condition and too fragile to be shifted. They looked fine as far as he was concerned. And besides, the longer she was here, the more chance someone would talk, someone would stumble on the news of the discovery, and the sharks and parasites of the media world would descend *en masse.* The story could break somewhere else—anywhere else; he didn't care—and then the media attention would be someone else's problem.

So he would tell her. And then she would go.

Nothing could be simpler.

The door to her office was slightly ajar. He pushed it open, still rehearsing his speech. It wouldn't be a long one. *Pack your things and be ready for the next boat*, was about the size of it. Still, knowing Dr Hunter and how she liked an argument, he was mentally preparing for a fight.

He was also preparing himself to win.

She was sitting at the desk, so intent on one of the pages she was studying and on the notes she was typing in the notebook computer alongside that she didn't hear him enter. She looked younger today, even with the frown puckering her brow, or maybe she just looked fresher. She'd dispensed with the ponytail and instead had twisted her hair behind her head so the blonde tips feathered out, and she'd swapped the khaki shirt for a white tank with straps so thin he wondered how they covered her bra straps.

Assuming she was wearing one...

Breath whooshed from his lungs. His blood rushed south.

She muttered something, still oblivious to his presence, and jumped out of her chair, wheeling around to the briefcase on the credenza beside her, rummaging through its contents. It would be rude to interrupt now, he thought, when she was so intensely involved in her work. Besides, the view from the back was no hardship to endure either. A well-worn denim skirt lovingly hugged her bottom and made his hands itch to do the same. But it was the length of the skirt he approved of most, or rather the lack of it, showcasing the surprisingly long legs beneath.

He sucked in air, desperate to replace what he had lost. She was nothing like the woman from the village. That woman was olive-skinned and dark-eyed, lush with curves and sultry good-looks. Whereas this one was blonde and petite, blue-eyed and more than slightly bookish. It made no sense.

Except for one more difference that made all the sense in the world.

This woman he wanted.

She pulled something from the briefcase then, a sheaf of papers, and looked up, blinking warily when she saw him standing in the doorway. 'Count Volta. I wasn't expecting you.'

He nodded. 'Dr Hunter,' he acknowledged, moving closer, searching his mind, certain that he'd been intending to say something but knowing only that he needed to get closer— maybe then it would come to him. And maybe he might even find an answer to his earlier question. But before he could latch onto his reason for coming, or work out whether there were telltale lines under her singlet after all, her face broke into one of those electric smiles. He felt the charge all the way to his toes, felt the jolt in his aching length.

'You picked the best time to drop by. Come and see.'

'What is it?'

'I translated the first of the pages. It's a prayer, a midnight prayer, beseeching the coming of dawn and an end to the darkness of night.'

He looked at the page and then at the translation she had up on her screen. 'And that's important because…?'

'Don't you see? The *Salus Totus* was revered—no, more than that, almost worshipped in its own right—as a book of healing. But little of the book remains to explain why. Remnants talk of eating and drinking in moderation, of taking fresh air, and while that is good advice, scholars have always felt there must have been more to warrant such a reputation for miracle cures and saved lives. Speculation has existed for centuries as to what might be in the missing pages and why they were removed.'

He didn't understand what she was getting at. He couldn't honestly say he cared. But her face was so animated with whatever she'd discovered that he could not help but join in the game. He shrugged. 'Because the pages offended someone they had to be destroyed?'

She shook her head. 'That's the most common theory, I agree, but I don't think it's right. Not now. I think they were sliced from the book not to destroy them but to save them.'

'Why?'

'Because they're secular. They're prayers of life and living that talk about the earth as mother of all. Nothing offensive to us now, in these times, but for all their gentle truths and wisdom they would have been seen as blasphemy then. The only reason we have what remains of the *Salus Totus* is because these pages were removed from inside its covers. With them gone there was no risk of offending anyone and the book could live on in more than memories. If they had stayed, the *Salus Totus* would surely have been thrown into the fires. So you see, by removing them from the book someone was trying to preserve them. Someone was trying to ensure their survival.'

Colour was high in her cheeks. Her blue eyes were so

bright they had a luminous quality. He didn't know anything about ancient texts or book-burning, but he knew *he* was burning and if he didn't do something soon he would self-combust. His hand found its way to her shoulder, scooped around to her nape, his fingers threading into the upward sweep of her hair. She blinked up at him, questions in her clear eyes to which he had no answers.

Except that he wanted her.

CHAPTER SIX

SHE trembled slightly as he dipped his mouth and brought her close, but it was not fear he sensed under his hand but an answering tremor of need. And then his lips touched hers and she sighed into his mouth. It was all he could do not to crush her to him. It was all he could do to remember to breathe. And when he did it was filled with the tantalising fresh perfume of her set amidst the coiling scent of desire.

He drew her closer, her lips soft under his own, pliant, her body close enough that they touched, chest to chest, her nipples hard against him. *No bra*, he registered with that small part of his brain still functioning, aching to fill his hands with her sweetness. Aching to fill her. Aching...

His hand cupped her behind, angling her back towards the desk, deepening the kiss as he lifted her.

She should not be doing this. She should have told him no. She had felt his warm hand slide around her neck, seen his mouth descend and known she should stop him.

Except she hadn't.

Just one taste, she'd foolishly thought, before she'd insist they stop. One taste of a man who could turn her inside out with just one heated glance. One taste of a man who made her feel more acutely aware of her gender and her innate femininity than she'd ever felt before.

And now, with his lips on hers, coaxing, bewitching, one

taste wasn't enough. One taste led to a hunger for more. He was addictive. Compelling. Impossible to deny.

Her body was his accomplice. Her skin rejoiced at his touch. Her mouth revelled in his mastery and his mystery.

Even when his hand slid to her behind, squeezed her and caused every muscle inside her to contract and then bloom, even when she felt a moment of panic and knew this was dangerous and foolhardy and reckless and so many of those things she had never been, she could not stop herself. For whatever he was awakening in her, whatever madness he was unleashing, she wanted more.

She gasped into his mouth and found no respite, for he claimed her lips in a savage kiss that fuelled her desires and quenched her now wafer-thin resistance. And, whatever he was doing, she knew it was well worth the price. For his kiss was a drug, pulling at her sensibilities, his touch on her flesh a sizzling brand.

Divorced from reality, she was his for the taking—almost. For when she felt his hands beneath her, lifting her, when she felt herself settled somewhere he could so deliciously insinuate his legs between hers, there came the tiniest glimmer of doubt—almost as if she'd lost hold of something she should remember in the firestorm of their mutual desire.

But no rational thought could find a way through this forbidden haze of primal need, and she gave herself up to the wanton pleasure of his hot mouth at her breast.

Until she reached back to steady herself against his pressing weight and felt her hand brush something aside—something featherlight that fluttered from the table.

She wrenched her mouth away from his, turned her head to see the centuries-old page flutter to the floor. With a mighty shove born of panic she pushed him away. 'What the hell are you thinking?'

The words were directed as much as to herself as to him. She was madder with herself, because she should have known better. What a fool! She swiped a glove from the box on her desk, pulling it on as she knelt down. If her actions had compromised the page's condition she might as well give up her job now. She would never forgive herself. Maybe she should give it up anyway, given she'd so easily disregarded her first responsibility. A paper that had survived for centuries only to be destroyed by a thoughtless couple behaving on top of it like hormone-driven teenagers—and one of them the person charged with ensuring its preservation. That would look good in her report. If she wanted to make a name for herself in this industry, a name nobody would ever forget, there would be no faster or surer way.

What the hell had she been thinking?

That was an easy one. Clearly she hadn't been thinking—not beyond her own carnal desires.

'It looks fine.'

Maybe to him. Nothing looked fine from her angle. Everything was off-kilter. Everything was wrong. She swiped sudden tears from her eyes, not sure if they stemmed from what had just so nearly happened on the desk or from relief that the page appeared to have survived its ordeal intact. But she was not about to risk dripping salty tears all over the page and add insult to injury. 'Just go, will you?'

She slid a folio beneath the page, lifting it gently back to the desk, using the opportunity to take a few more steps and put the desk between them at the same time. She would have to check the page for materials and fibres picked up from the rug, but pulling out her tweezers and microscope would have to wait until the Count had gone and her hands had stopped shaking.

'Dr Hunter…'

'Haven't you done enough? I asked you to go.'

His jaw firmed, his eyes grew hard edged. 'You're blaming me?'

'I certainly didn't kiss *you*!'

'No? I distinctly remember there were two of us there. And I sure as hell don't remember anyone complaining.'

She squeezed her eyes shut, remembering only too well her lack of resistance. 'I think we both made a mistake. And now, if you don't mind, I have work to do.' She curled her hands into fists, willing the shaking to stop, trying to make sense of this unfamiliar recklessness and get her scientific self back together while he loomed there, her very own dark cloud.

'Have dinner with me tonight.'

Her breath caught. Dinner—*and what else?* Why the sudden hospitality? Unless he was looking to finish what he'd started?

'I'm not sure that's such a good idea.'

'You have to eat.'

'I'm very good at eating alone. Luckily, as it happens.'

'If that's a dig at the way you've been treated here—'

'Take it how you like. But I live alone. I'm good with it.'

He regarded her coolly from under hooded lids. 'You're afraid.'

'I'm not afraid of you. It's just that I don't see the point. Every time we're together we end up arguing or—'

His chin lifted, a spark glinted in his eyes. 'You are afraid we will not argue?'

'Should I be?'

'I think whether or not we argue is something that is as much up to you as it is to me.'

And that was *exactly* what she was afraid of. One kiss and she'd forgotten who she even was. How could something as mechanical as the meeting of two mouths do that? She'd had lovers before, and neither of them had come close to making her feel anything like this man did. Okay, so maybe her first time had been more clinical than exciting, and borne of desperation that she would be the sole virgin in her university graduating class, and the second time had been grief sex with a colleague after a child she'd nursed for days in the refugee hospital had died in her arms. It had been bitter and sweet and life-affirming and exactly what she'd needed at the time, but it had been nothing to rival the impact of even this man's kiss.

Dared she dine with him? If he kissed her again, how would she resist? And with what? She had no defences against such an onslaught. If she even wanted to stop it. She hadn't before, and if that paper hadn't fallen to the floor what would they be doing now? She shuddered and squeezed her eyes shut, but it didn't stop the images dancing in her mind's eye. Right there, *on the desk.*

'You can tell me more of your theories,' he prompted, clearly sensing her waver, 'and perhaps I can share mine about why the pages might have ended up here under the castle.'

He had a theory? She looked up. She wanted to hear that. She just wasn't certain about the *you-show-me-yours-and-I'll-show-you-mine* subtext. 'Or,' she countered, 'you could just tell me now.'

'But you have work to do, my dear Dr Hunter. And I have already disturbed you enough.'

True, but he would continue to disturb her whether or not he was here—now more than ever. 'Look,' she said, shaking her head, knowing it would be crazy to expect they could dine together and pretend that kiss had never happened. She gestured down at her casual singlet and skirt. 'I didn't expect to be entertained. I brought nothing—'

'On the contrary,' he interjected, 'you look charming. But if it pleases you I'm sure we can find you something you will be more comfortable in.'

She sighed, knowing she was fighting a losing battle. Of course he was sure to have an entire women's wardrobe at his disposal. Or maybe Bruno was also a fine seamstress. 'Fine,' she said in resignation, just wanting more than ever to get back to her work. There was an outside chance she could finish up the translations today, and if she did that, given the excellent condition of the pages, there was no reason why she couldn't leave early and finish the rest of her report elsewhere. She had contacts in any number of universities across Europe that had the right facilities and who would be delighted to play host to such a famous text. And he wanted her gone. Surely she could survive just one meal together? 'Fine. In that case I'd be delighted to join you for dinner.'

His eyes glinted with victory. 'It is a long time since I had the pleasure of a beautiful woman as my dinner companion.'

'You don't have to resort to flattery, Count Volta. I have already said I'd come.'

'Alessandro,' he said, with a nod and a smile at her acquiescence. 'And I shall call you Grace. I think we can drop the formalities, don't you?' He bowed his head and finally headed for the door. 'Until dinner, then.'

She nodded absently, turning back to her work, knowing she should be concentrating on that rather than replaying the sound of his name in her head.

Alessandro.

Oh, no. She didn't like that. She didn't want to give him a name. She didn't want to think of him as Alessandro. She preferred to think of him as the Count. It made him sound remote. A little unreal.

Whereas Alessandro made him sound almost human. It made him sound like a man.

And she didn't want to think of him as a man.

'Oh, and Grace?'

She blinked and looked around. 'Yes?'

'That wasn't flattery.'

He had her. He strode back to his office, knowing that tonight she would grace both his table and his bed. She was as good as his. And tonight, and for all the nights that she remained here, he would have her. Nothing surer.

He almost growled in anticipation. He didn't understand this need, this compulsion to have her. He hated strangers. And yet he wanted her more than he had ever wanted anything before in his life.

Did it matter why?

Wasn't it enough to know that he wanted her and that she was his for the taking? And by the time she left he would have rid himself of whatever spell this was that she had cast over him—rid himself of this compulsion to bed her and to watch the sparks in her eyes, to feel the electricity inside her as she came apart around him.

He could hardly wait.

CHAPTER SEVEN

GRACE rubbed her eyes and leaned back in her chair, a bubble of excitement glowing pearlescent and pretty as her raw theory took shape and substance—a bubble only slightly tainted by a niggling concern that she had missed something.

She couldn't quite put her finger on it. Her supposition that the pages had been removed to protect them rather than to destroy them wasn't just a rash idea now; the pages she had translated since then only lent weight to her theory.

One page had been in praise of mothers and motherhood and the sacred mother-child bond. Another had been a celebration of spring and renewal in all things spiritual and physical. Another an endorsement of acting kindly to friends and strangers alike. All of them fabulous. All of them a revelation into thoughts based more on humanitarian principles rather than the dictates of any particular religion. That would have been crime enough to have them destroyed.

But it was the last page that gave the most credence to her theory.

It was probably the most spectacular of all the pages. The inks were fresh and clear, the colours almost leaping from the page, bold and beautiful. It was the message that disturbed her on some deep, uncomfortable level.

It warned of an affliction with no cure. An odd subject, Grace had thought, in a so-called book of healing, assuming it must contain a description of a disease beyond the range of a physician's treatment. Cancer, or any number of things that would have been similarly incurable back then.

The affliction was random, the scribe warned, regardless of wealth or station. It was ruthless and devastating in its impact.

It must be something like cancer, she'd mused as she'd made notes before continuing. But, reading on, she'd realised she'd been wrong.

It made your chest thump and left you breathless and weak. It turned your mind to a porridge filled with poems and songs and other, darker, carnal longings. And should you fall you were doomed, and no god in heaven or on earth could save you. Yet if you succumbed you were the most blessed soul alive.

Love, Grace had realised with a smile, working through the translation. Love was the scribe's fatal affliction, its victims both doomed and blessed. She'd heard plenty of modern ballads with similar themes. It never ceased to amaze her how some things transcended not only the generations but the centuries.

Still, something bothered her. She checked her notes, unable to dispel the glimmer of uneasiness. But there was nothing untoward that she could see, and anyway it was time to pack up and get dressed for dinner.

She gathered her things, sending up silent thanks to whoever it was who had removed the pages from the book for safekeeping all those centuries ago. Soon, if all went well and her findings were corroborated, the pages and the book would be reunited.

And tomorrow she could leave. Her heart gave a little lurch she interpreted as relief. Already she felt better about dinner, more in control. The doctor was back in charge, her earlier recklessness put aside. Dinner would be fine, she told herself. She'd tell him what she'd found and ask him about why he thought the pages had ended up here. She'd tell him she was leaving and ask him to arrange transport. What could possibly happen when she was leaving tomorrow?

She returned to her bedroom. Gloomy light was filtering

into the room courtesy of the dark clouds hiding the sun. Wind rattled at the windows. Another rough night, she presumed, the scientist in her firmly back in control. There was nothing sinister about it. Stormy nights were just the way things were here.

But the weather faded to insignificance when she turned on the light and saw what was waiting for her on the bed.

It was a gown of liquid silk, a waterfall of blue and green rippling over the coverlet, and it was the most glorious thing she had ever seen. She held it up against herself and realised it was new, its store tag swinging free. A store she'd never been game enough to walk into in her life. It must have cost a fortune. How on earth had he found it?

Ten minutes later, showered and fresh, she slipped it on. It floated over her skin, setting it alight like a lover's caress, reminding her of the sensation when Alessandro's big hands had skimmed over her. She shivered with the memories, turning this way and that in the mirror, trying to focus on what she saw and put out of her mind what she remembered. The one-shouldered design fitted perfectly, its silk feeling magical against her skin. She loved what she saw. Spinning around in front of the mirror, her inner girl delighted. She never wore pretty things. It was usually jeans or a denim skirt for work, and practical suits for presentations to libraries or at conferences. She owned one whole cocktail dress. Black, of course. Never in her life had she worn something so utterly—*feminine*.

She coiled her hair—nothing special, with loose tendrils refusing to behave and escaping, but it would have to do. She applied what little make-up she'd bothered to bring and stepped into the silver sandals left with the dress and made one final check in the mirror.

Would he approve? She hoped so. And immediately wondered why it even mattered what he thought. She was leaving tomorrow. Still, she thought, with a flutter in her tummy as she headed for the dining room, he always looked so regal in his high-collared suits. It would be nice to appear for once in something less casual. And it would be gratifying if he at least approved.

He had the hard-on from hell. One look at the vision that had just entered the room and it was a wonder it hadn't bodily dragged him across the room. God, but he wanted her!

He forced his hungry mouth into a smile as he poured her a glass of champagne. 'You look—ravishing.'

She actually blushed, and stumbled delightfully over something she'd been going to say, ratcheting up his hunger tenfold. Was she so unused to compliments? She was a goddess in that dress, needing no jewellery when her blue eyes sparkled like sapphires. And if she was a goddess in it, he couldn't wait to see her out of it.

Soon, he assured the ravenous beast bucking for release. *Soon*.

'The dress is lovely, thank you.' She headed uncertainly towards him, taking the circuitous way round as if interested in the photographs lining the mantelpiece in the grand high-ceilinged room. She had to watch what she said. When he'd told her she looked ravishing she'd almost said, *So do you.*

But it was true. In another of those high-collared jackets, that fitted him like a second skin and showed off the tapering of shoulders to hip to magnificent effect, he looked like royalty.

He *was* royalty, she reminded herself. A count. With connections that went back for ever. Which reminded her of much safer territory than how good he looked right now...

'Did you want to tell me about that theory of yours? About how the pages might have ended up in the caves below your castle?'

He handed her a glass of sparkling gold-tinged liquid and their fingers brushed, causing an electric jolt to her senses and her heart. The silver shoes, she figured, preferring to blame static electricity than take heed of the niggling worm of doubt lurking in the back of her mind.

He smiled down at her, as if he'd sensed her sudden discomfiture, and she was forced to meet his eyes and pretend unconcern, closing her lips before she could tell him he smelt ravishing as well, clean and masculine and all too addictive.

'Pirates,' he said simply.

She blinked up at him, lost in his scent, trying to regain hold of the conversation. 'Why would pirates care about a few random pages cut from a book? Wouldn't they be more interested in treasure and looting?'

'Perhaps they didn't care about the pages themselves, but the money they were paid to hide them. They would know where to secrete them to keep them safe from prying eyes. The caves beneath this castle were used by pirates for centuries, even while the first Counts were in residence. Perhaps someone paid them to find somewhere safe—somewhere the authorities would never find them. Somewhere they didn't know the location of themselves.'

'So they could never give it away if anyone asked…' Her mind was working through the possibilities. 'They must have known they could be lost and might never be found.'

'It was no doubt a better option than to be burned outright. Little would have existed of the *Salus Totus* then.'

She looked up at him. 'You sound like you care—like the *Salus Totus* really matters to you. Why do you care about these pages? You could have left them there and not told anyone. Nobody would have been any the wiser.'

Before he could answer the door swung open on Bruno pushing a trolley.

'Ah, dinner is served,' the Count said with a smile. 'Please be seated.'

He put a hand to the small of her back to direct her, and she felt warmth and heat and an instant connection. It was utterly innocent, she was sure, and the fabric of her dress was separating them, and yet she had never felt anything quite so shockingly intimate. Did he have any idea what that low touch did to her? How it stirred her in secret places and moved her to remember a kiss that had near wrenched her soul as well as her defences away?

She swallowed, some of her earlier confidence trickling away. She was leaving tomorrow but that still left tonight. Why had she thought it would be such a breeze? What if he'd planned dinner to be one long assault to her senses? The brush of his fingers when he'd handed her the glass, the touch of his fingers to her back—was it all part of a long, sweet seduction?

He leaned over her as she was seated and she felt his warm breath stir the ends of her hair and brush her ear. She shuddered, suddenly breathless and flushed and trying to ignore the thrum of blood in her veins.

She was reminded of that line of the translation…

'It makes your chest thump and leaves you breathless.'

Where had that come from?

No. That was laughable. Ridiculous. Although her brain must certainly be turning to porridge if she entertained any such thoughts!

'It is random, regardless of wealth or station.'

That proved nothing. She was tired, overwrought after a long couple of days, and the lines were fresh in her mind.

'It turns your mind to a porridge filled with poems and songs and other, darker, carnal longings.'

There! Not once had she felt inclined to burst into song or break out a sonnet. And she wasn't the type to have dark, carnal longings. Even if just a tiny fraction of her wondered about his hard body and how it would feel to have him inside her. If that paper hadn't fallen, if they hadn't stopped…

Her body hummed with unfamiliar awareness. A pulse she'd never known existed made itself known and almost ached…

'Is something wrong?'

The room came back into focus. She noticed the delicate porcelain bowl in front of her and the scent of wild mushroom and herbs from the soup someone had ladled into it. And she noticed him, watching her. Somewhere along the line her appetite for food had disappeared, been replaced with an appetite for something else entirely.

Lust, she thought. She hadn't had much personal experience but she guessed that could be a chronic affliction too. But not necessarily fatal. Definitely temporary. She'd start feeling better as soon as she'd left the island.

'It's been a long day,' she offered. 'I'm sorry. I'm probably not very good company tonight.'

'Did you have trouble with your work today?'

'No. On the contrary, I managed to cover a lot more than I expected. In fact, I was going to talk to you about that. I've got enough done that I don't need to trouble you any more. I'm hoping the boat can pick me up tomorrow morning.'

The atmosphere flat-lined between them.

'Tomorrow.'

It wasn't a question. More an accusation.

'Yes. Will it be a problem to get the boat, do you think? Only the pages are in such good condition they are more than safe for transportation, and I can continue my studies and complete my report elsewhere before the discovery goes public.'

'You're going to leave?'

She blinked. 'Isn't that what you want? For me to be gone as soon as possible?'

Yes!

But not this way. Not this soon. Not now! 'How can you be sure there's nothing more to learn here? What is the point of rushing elsewhere?'

Escape.

'I'll just have to take that risk.' There would be more to learn, she knew it. She would love to investigate the tunnels beneath the castle some more, to learn more of their shadowy past, but there was no way she'd trust herself down there with him again. 'I'll make my report. Others might want to fill in more details and undertake a research trip later.'

'I don't want *others* here!'

'That's not my problem!'

A flash of lightning rent the skies and shook the very foundations. A boom of thunder followed hot on its heels, along with a burst of rain splattering against the windows.

'Is it always stormy at night here?' she asked him, when the rolling boom had finally died away, breathless with the shock of the onslaught.

'Not always.' He was leaning back in his chair, his jaw set, his eyes as hard as the rock this castle was constructed with. He picked up his spoon. 'Sometimes it's stormy during the day too.'

Lovely. Clearly she'd visited the castle in the high season. She followed his lead, only to toy with her spoon, barely tasting the soup. She'd known they would either argue or end up in each other's arms and more. Clearly it would not be the latter tonight.

Which was a good thing, wasn't it?

She had no intention of ending up in his bed. Even if she was leaving tomorrow and the idea of a one-night affair came with a frisson of the forbidden. One night with a dark count with a savage heart. One night of passion unleashed.

Utter recklessness, she told herself, shifting a little in her chair. Of course she didn't want that.

Bruno grunted when he made to clear away her plate. 'Not finished?'

'Thank you, it was lovely. I'm not really that hungry.' She smiled up at him, wondering if he ever smiled. 'Does Bruno do the cooking too?' she asked as he disappeared with their plates, looking for a safer topic to discuss.

'Of course not.' Alessandro almost snapped the words,

seemed to think twice and made another effort. 'Of course I have a cook.'

'Oh, I think I saw her. A pretty dark-haired girl?'

'You saw her?'

'I happened to see the boat come in earlier today. She was on it. I thought she must work at the castle.'

A muscle in his jaw twitched. 'My cook is named Pietro. There are no women who work at the castle.'

'Oh.'

He didn't volunteer who the woman was and she wasn't about to ask. Maybe she should have picked another topic. An antique mantel clock rang out the hour and then fell silent again. She studied her hands, busy tying themselves into knots in her lap, while outside the rain continued to come down. It would clear tomorrow, she reassured herself, just like it had cleared today.

Right now the boat couldn't come soon enough.

Somehow, stiffly, they made it through the rest of the courses, and Grace was never more grateful than when coffee was served. Conversation had been stilted and terse and limited to little more than the likes of, 'How is your duck?' and, 'Lovely, thank you.'

It had been an ordeal rather than a meal. She knew he was angry with her, but what she couldn't work out was why. He'd been the one to make her feel unwelcome from the start. He'd been the one who'd insisted she leave as soon as she was finished. And now he was acting as if she was cutting and running. And now he was the one who glowered at her with those dark eyes until she shivered with the intensity of it all.

What was his problem?

'It's late,' she said. 'I should get my things packed.'

'Of course,' he said, standing as she rose. 'You will forgive me, Dr Hunter, if I do not see you off in the morning. Bruno will collect your things and take you to the boat.'

Something lurched inside her—something beyond the unexpected hurt of him dropping the Grace and resuming use of her title. So this would be the last time she'd see him? How strange that felt, when she'd been expecting relief.

'Thank you, Count Volta. Both for your hospitality and for returning the lost pages of the *Salus Totus* to the world. I will be sure to accord your contribution due recognition in my report.'

He gave a slight bow, formal and brief. 'Goodnight, Dr Hunter.'

She was halfway to the door when he called her, and she turned uncertainly, unable to prevent or understand the tiny bubble of hope that came with his call. 'Yes?'

'Take the dress when you go,' he said. 'I have no use for it.'

She knew she shouldn't be disappointed. He'd made it clear he was angry with her. But she would take the dress. She doubted she would ever have cause to wear it, but she would treasure it for ever. 'Thank you. I meant to ask—wherever did it come from?'

His eyes looked back at her, bleak and soulless. 'It was my fiancée's.'

She was leaving. He sat at the empty table, a hint of her perfume the only remaining trace of her.

She was leaving.

Somehow he'd made it through the dinner, forcing food into a body already shutting down.

She was leaving. And, beyond locking her in a turret room or throwing her into the caves below the castle, he had no choice but to let her go.

He'd always intended to let her go.

She did not belong here.

She did not belong to him.

But, God, he had not planned on losing her so soon.

The blackness was there, lurking in the fringes of his mind, bubbling away like boiling mud and fouling the air with stinking gases. It was there and mocking him for letting her go, ready to claim him again. He'd thought there was a chance of...

He searched helplessly to latch onto what he was looking for. He didn't know.

Only that he had come to recognise she offered a chance of something—a chance to reclaim what he'd once had, a chance to reconnect to a world of light instead of dark. He wanted to at least taste that light.

And after a decade of burying himself away in the dark he'd seen that light in her expression and lusted after it for himself.

Just a taste.

Was that too much to ask?

Clearly too much. And so he'd pulled back before she could further cut him loose. He'd withdrawn into his dark state to preserve what little of himself there was left.

He'd hurt her in the process.

He'd seen her stricken face when he'd told her about the dress. He'd sensed the trembling under her pale skin before she'd fled in a flurry of blue silk on a wavering goodnight.

Why had he told her that?

Payback? Because she'd teased him with the taste of something he'd long given up on, only to deprive him of it when he'd been lured under her spell? Because she'd reminded him of his failure with the village woman he'd sent packing because he wanted her instead?

Or maybe just because he'd finally become that monster he'd always been made out to be?

Because that dress had been made to be worn, and even if Adele had ever deigned to select it from her extensive wardrobe it would never have looked half as good as it had tonight on Dr Grace Hunter.

Why hadn't he told her that instead?

He knew why.

Because she was leaving tomorrow.

CHAPTER EIGHT

SHE should have thought to bring something to wrap around herself. She was almost frozen by the time she returned to her room. And it wasn't just the storm outside and the wind that wailed a mournful song outside that turned her skin to goosebumps. It was the dreadfulness of dinner and the anti-climax of it all. She was chilled from the inside out.

She was leaving tomorrow. She should feel relieved.

And yet instead she felt this massive let-down.

Hormones, she told herself, or the sudden lack of them. The post-adrenaline rush. Nothing more scientific than that.

But still…

She unzipped the dress and let it slide from her body, letting it pool on the floor at her feet.

His fiancée's dress.

She shivered anew. God, what that had done to her. A dress chosen by the woman he had loved. The woman who had died that night along with so many others all those years long ago. Why had he wanted her to wear it?

She collapsed onto the bed and buried her face in her hands while the wind outside howled her distress.

She took a deep breath to steady herself. It was okay. She was leaving in the morning. Everything would be fine in the morning.

Like an automaton she packed her belongings to the sounds of a storm that mirrored her mood perfectly—every clap of thunder cheered, every burst of rain celebrated. The packing took nowhere near long enough for the storm. Her tools she'd already cleaned and packed. The pages were secure in acid-free packaging, padded to protect them from bumps during transit. There was nothing for it but to sleep and pray the storm had blown itself out by morning.

And the dress? She left it on a hanger in the dressing room before she slipped between the covers and settled her head into the pillows. It was a beautiful gown, there was no doubt—more exotic, more expensive than anything she had ever seen before or could ever afford—and she'd felt a million dollars inside its silken drapes. But it wasn't hers.

It would never be truly hers.

It was dark when she awoke, disorientated and confused after another fitful sleep and wondering again what had roused her. At first she thought it must be just that the wind had dropped and the rain had ceased, the lull leaving everything suddenly almost unnaturally quiet.

Until she heard it. The sound wound almost hauntingly through the night air until it was carried away with the next gust of wind.

She sat up. Definitely notes from a piano. Maybe she hadn't imagined it last night after all.

Between gusts of wind she caught more snatches, the notes melancholy and slightly off-beat, increasing in parts. Bewitching.

She snapped on her light, relieved the power was still on, saw that it was two in the morning and listened, wondering where it was coming from. The music had moved to a more comforting melody, undulating and lyrical, soft and warm, except there were gaps and she hated that she kept missing bits—hated that they were carried away on the wind. Then rain splattered against her windows, drowning out the sound entirely.

Intrigued, she slid from between the covers, drawing on her robe. If she opened her door just a little she might hear more over the weather.

The door snicked open and light spilled into the shadow-filled passageway. She listened. It was coming from somewhere downstairs. The rain intensified, thunder rumbled overhead and the poignant notes were lost again. She took a step towards the stairs, and then another, barefoot and silent in the darkened hallway.

She reached the top of the stairs and peered down into the inky depths. The music was hauntingly beautiful and yet so utterly, utterly wretched. And she felt compelled to hear more.

She looked around the darkened empty hall, nervous and excited at the same time. Nobody would see her, and if they did surely there was no crime in listening? Still, she took the steps gingerly, the haunting notes luring her further and further down. It was coming from the ballroom that, from the impression she'd gained in her brief time here, seemed to take up one half of the massive frontage of the castle.

With no light to guide her, with the music leading her feet, she silently descended the stairway, hesitating on that final step as the rich emotion of the piece washed over her. It was building now, in time with the storm outside, a rising of passion that left her gasping at its intensity. She took one tentative step closer to the wide French doors leading into the ballroom, and then another, until she could see inside.

She didn't need light to know it was him. Even through the night-filled room, even across the yawning space between them, there was no mistaking the dark shadow at the piano, no mistaking it was pain he was feeling as he poured himself into the piece. She felt it too—felt that pain, felt that loss and his constant struggle.

And she fought with herself as she felt her own heart go out to this man. He had clearly lost so much.

He could be cruel, she reminded herself, remembering the

dress and the cold way he'd told her it was his fiancée's. He was autocratic. Imperious. Cold.

He'd wanted her gone and then he'd frozen her out when she'd told him she would be.

And that was after he'd practically forced himself upon her.

Except that he hadn't...

He'd kissed her and she'd responded in the only way she'd been able—by responding in kind, by kissing him back. Because, so help her, she'd wanted him then and it hadn't even occurred to her to stop him. And she wouldn't have if it hadn't been for that paper. She would have opened her legs and welcomed him.

She swallowed, her mouth suddenly dry, aching in that hollow space between her thighs. How could she judge him?

The notes rang out, fighting the storm raging outside for supremacy, frenetic as the passion burst into a climax of such frenzied intensity that tears sprang unbidden to her eyes. A flash of lightning lit the room and displayed him in all his tragic beauty, his pain and torment clear in every stark feature and the scarred plane of his cheek.

The room went dark as the music crashed so suddenly down to earth that she held her breath and nearly turned and ran lest he discover her there, watching him.

Except that before her feet would move the notes resumed, almost from nowhere, soft and melodic. She recognised the earlier tune, only sweeter this time, and more poignant if that were possible. The notes tumbled like a stream, light and magical and so evocative that tears spilled down her cheeks.

She watched him as much as the storm-ridden night allowed as he coaxed honeyed sweetness from the instrument so that it almost bent to his will, compliant as a new lover willing to please—until he changed direction and willed it to insanity once again, urging it higher and wilder until the notes meshed one final time with the storm outside, only to collapse and shudder to a dramatic conclusion.

She heard the piano lid bang closed. She heard breathing, loud and close, and froze, panicked, only to realise it was her own ragged breaths she was hearing. She cursed herself for the time she had lost in making her escape.

She'd wheeled around, trying to make sense of the dark shadows before her, when light flooded the room—a chandelier of one thousand tiny globes above turning night to day.

'Was there something you wanted, Dr Hunter?'

Adrenaline flushed through her veins. Her heart pounded frantically in her chest as she surveyed the stairs. Escape was right there, brilliantly and starkly illuminated, and yet her feet remained frozen to the floor. She dragged in air and pulled her robe tighter around her before she was game to turn around, trembling with panic and guilt at being caught out, knowing he would not welcome her intrusion.

'I heard music, Count Volta. I was curious.'

He was standing near the doorway, wearing the same suit he'd worn at their disastrous dinner, as formal and regal as ever, though his eyes seemed darker and even more tortured if that were possible. 'I hope I did not disturb your sleep.'

No more than usual. 'No. Really, I was…' She swiped at a wayward tear on her cheek. 'I was just getting up for a glass of—' His dark eyes narrowed and she forgot what she had been going to say as he came closer, his eyes missing nothing as he took in the robe and the tightly cinched belt.

'But you have been crying.'

'The music,' she said. 'It was so beautiful. I'm sorry. I'll…'

But he was already wiping away the moisture with the pad of his thumb—so tenderly, so at odds with the dark, tortured eyes that raked her face, that more tears squeezed free. There was a tightness to his features. His face was set almost like a mask. It was a tightness that spoke of anger and resentment and some barely controlled agony.

A tightness that frightened her and yet excited her on some primeval level, just as his touch set her skin alight. 'It is late,' he said tightly, his fingers resting lightly on her cheek. 'You should be in bed if you are leaving tomorrow.'

'I'll go now,' she whispered, wondering if he might stop her. Half wanting him to.

'I'll see you to your room.'

'I'll be fine.' She had to get away. She couldn't stand the tension of having him walk alongside her, wondering all the way, back to her room. She couldn't stand the disappointment if he merely left her at the door and walked away. 'I know the way.'

She turned back, her feet programmed now to flee, only for the storm to unleash one more act of savagery. The boom crashed overhead and reverberated through the floor and walls. For a split second the room was still lit with the light from the chandelier, only to plunge the next instant into blackness so thick it was like a wall.

Panicked, she plunged into it, only to trip against the first step—would have fallen if he hadn't been there first to gather her into his arms.

Air was knocked from her lungs, and when she breathed again the air came full of the heady scent of him. His arms were like iron bars around her, powerful and strong, as slowly he righted her until her feet touched the ground. Her knees buckled and his arms tightened, pulling her against the hard wall of his chest.

She heard his ragged breathing, she could feel the pounding of his heart in his chest, and she didn't need light to tell her he was looking at her. She knew by the intoxicating fan of his breath against her face and by the sheer intensity of his stillness. She knew by the sudden fullness of her breasts and the aching tightness of her nipples.

'You are leaving tomorrow,' he said, sounding almost as if he was reminding himself, trying to convince himself.

'Yes.' Her word was no more than a whispered breath, and she sensed rather than saw the shake of his head.

'You should not have come downstairs.' His voice was choked and thick, and a shudder rippled deep and evocative through her. 'You should not have come.'

His words were warm and rich and scented with the unmistakable essence of him and she drank him in, tasting him. 'I had no choice,' she admitted, her lips hungry and searching the darkness. 'You gave me no choice.'

He made a sound, strangled and thick, as her drew her closer, her head cradled in his hands. 'I am giving you a choice now. Tell me, before I give way to the monster inside me and decide for you, what do you want?'

Her heart lurched. Her senses lurched. His hands were hot on her face and in her hair as he waited for her answer. Her skin was alive with the touch of him, her body alight with need, and right now there was only one answer. Lust, she told herself, feeling herself falling further from reality and the safe world she had always known, the safe person she had always been. But she was leaving in the morning. Was one stolen night too much to ask?

And she put her hands over his, lacing their fingers together. 'I want you.'

Lightning flashed. Thunder boomed. And the room was suddenly so bright she was surprised she couldn't see her need splashed right across the ceiling.

But she could see him. Saw the flames flare in his eyes as his mouth crashed down on hers. And she knew she was lost. His kiss was wrenching at her very soul just like the music had done, reaching inside her to unleash emotions she'd never known existed. His mouth was setting her alight, his touch sending her skin aflame.

And then, still kissing her, she was in his arms as he mounted the stairs two at a time, with a speed that she would normally consider reckless but which now felt strangely necessary. Because she wanted him. Burned for him.

She didn't know where he was taking her in the dark. She didn't care whose bed it was he laid her down upon. She only cared that soon he would soon quench this aching need. This burning desire.

Her fingers scrabbled with his jacket, protesting at the barrier, and without leaving her mouth he ripped it off and let it fall to the floor. He tugged loose her robe while her hands clawed at his shoulders, wanting him back, wanting to feel him against her. She forgave him when she felt his palms sliding from her thighs to her breasts, drawing her nightgown upwards with it. She lifted her head to let it go while his fingers trailed back down her body.

'Beautiful,' he growled, leaning over her, rolling one tight nipple under his thumb and making her back arch into the bed. 'Do you know how much I want you?'

'Please,' she implored, desperate now. Nobody had ever called her beautiful. Nobody had ever told her they wanted her. And now his words fuelled a body already screaming for release. Her hands were at his waist and then below, until she gasped into his mouth as she discovered exactly how much he wanted her, her fingers marvelling, tracing his rigid length.

He groaned like an animal in distress and grabbed the offending wrist, pinning it to the bed while he freed himself with the other and ripped open protection with his teeth. *Surely now!*

But still she had to wait. 'Please!' she cried when his hand peeled away her panties, his fingers slipping between her folds and brushing that tiny nub that seemed the repository of every nerve-ending she'd ever possessed while his mouth suckled one peaked breast.

She bucked into the bed and cried out with the sheer ecstasy of it, cried out with the unfairness of it all when his fingers teased her cleft. It was something else she wanted, something else she needed.

She curled her fingers in his hair, dragged his head from her breast. *'Please!'*

And then she felt him there, at her entrance, felt his heated pressure and his power and wondered for just one second if she was dreaming and at any moment she was going to wake up alone in twisted sheets, feeling cheated and unsatisfied.

A bolt of lightning rent the skies above, turning night into day, and her body yearned with pleasure unbound. And he was there, poised above her. 'You're so beautiful,' he murmured in the storm-light, his voice so tight with longing that it hurt to hear the words—until he stilled and entered her on one long, deep thrust that stretched her, filling her so completely, so perfectly—*so magically*—that she cried out with the wonderment of it all.

He was inside her, part of her. Every cell in her body was aware of his presence, shimmering with sensation. And then he started to withdraw, and lights exploded behind her eyes.

He gasped at their joining, taking just a moment to savour the exquisite tightness around him. He could feel her pulse in the slick flesh that sheathed him, could feel her muscles stretching to accommodate him, and he feared he would not last. And then he moved inside her and felt her buck beneath him, her muscles tighten around him, and he *knew* he could not last.

Lightning flashed overhead, thunder rumbled, and he pounded into her as the hail pounded at the windows. His own storm was building, and the woman beneath him was like a cyclone herself, wild and unpredictable as she thrashed below, urging his storm to intensify with her slick heat and electric spasms, until with a booming cry he exploded into her.

The lightning captured the moment, and he saw her up-turned face alight with wonderment, her blue eyes bright like stars. And even when the room was plunged into blackness again he felt the force of that light all around him.

It would not last. It could not last. She would go and once again the blackness and the bleakness would return. But for now he would live in the light.

He collapsed on top of her until his breathing was less ragged, his pounding heart quieted. Then he peeled himself away. 'You cried out,' he said. 'Did I hurt you?' He slipped her supine form in between the covers.

'No,' she whispered. 'It was—amazing.'

And he could hear her face light up in her words. He leaned over and kissed her before ridding himself of his shoes and trousers and climbing in alongside her.

She snuggled into him when he joined her, sighing against his shoulder, her hand sliding over his shirt. 'Why did you leave your shirt on?'

'Because the lights will come on some time.'

'You don't want me to see you?'

He remembered the look of revulsion on the village woman's face. 'You don't want to see me.'

Her fingers made lazy circles on his chest. 'I see your face.'

He caught her hand then, squeezed it briefly and let it go. 'You do. But this is much worse.'

Her hand skimmed his chest, drinking in the width and hardness of him, running down the length of his arm. She wanted to know everything about him. She wanted to be able to remember it all when she was gone. So soon she would be gone.

So little time...

Unless the storm continued? But the rain was no more than a sprinkle now against the windows, and the wind had blown itself out. The clouds were clearing enough for thin moonlight to slant over the bed.

'What time will the boat come?'

Never, he wanted to say, wanting to keep her here for ever, to hold onto her light. But she had to go. She wanted to go and present the lost pages to the world. She wanted the fame the discovery and her theories would bring.

And he had no right to beauty.

'Early,' he said. Her trailing fingers were stirring him, making him hard, so he caught them and showed her, unaccustomedly delighted with her small mewl of pleasure and the tentative exploration of her fingers. 'We'd better not waste any more time.'

He took much longer this time, none of it wasted. He took longer to pleasure every part of her with his hands and his mouth and his tongue, bringing her apart until she screamed with release before he pulled her astride him and lowered her slowly down his aching length.

God, she felt good as she rode him. Moonlight slanted across her body, turning her pale skin silver, her high breasts tipped with pink. She was a goddess and he was a monster.

And she was leaving in the morning.

She cried out as he flipped her onto her back, still inside her. *She was leaving.* He powered into her, pouring his frustrations and anger and desolation into every lunge, and she met him blow for blow, bucking under him, urging him on, her hips angled higher to take him deeper, her teeth at his shoulder, her hands clawing into his back and tangled in his shirt as the storm inside her built again. With one final thrust he sent her screaming into the abyss. She contracted around him, sparking and sizzling with electricity, and he had choice but to follow her as he pumped his own release.

They collapsed together as the first thin grey of dawn peeked through the windows. Vaguely he was aware of the buttons that had been wrenched away. Vaguely he knew he should do something before he fell asleep. But his arms were so heavy, and she was so warm and soft in his embrace, and the air was thick with the musky scent of their lovemaking. He would do something in just a while.

CHAPTER NINE

SHE woke with a start, disorientated and wondering where she was, until she remembered she'd fallen asleep in his arms not that many hours ago. Bright light now poured through the windows—the kind of light, she reflected sadly, that heralded sunny skies and an absence of storms. The kind of day, she cursed, just perfect to take a boat ride.

She could hear his steady breathing behind her and eased herself over to look at him. Had they really done all the things she remembered? Oh, yes, they had, she realised, if the unfamiliar aches in her body were any indication.

And then she saw him.

He was lying on his back, the shirt she remembered tearing apart in the height of passion open, exposing his chest to her gaze. She'd got just a hint of his injuries last night when her fingertips had grazed a ridge or encountered an unexpected dip under his shirt.

Now the ridges and dips made sense. Whatever had sliced into his face had dug deep into his chest as well, and then something more terrible had happened. It looked as if the left side of his chest had been blown apart and roughly patched together in some kind of ugly puckered design, brutal and savage. It looked as if whatever had blown his life apart had blown his chest apart with the same brutal effect. It looked so damaged that she ached with knowing what it must have cost.

'I told you that you didn't want to see it.'

She looked at him. Saw him watching her from under hooded lids, his eyes guarded as if he was waiting for her, almost challenging her to look away as he made no attempt to cover himself up. 'What happened? I read that your boat exploded, but how did this happen?'

'This was metal flying through the air,' he said, indicating the long line from his face to his chest. 'And this mess came courtesy of burning oil.'

She shuddered, imagining the horror and the pain. Unable to come anywhere close. And then, because she could find no words that would express anything that would help, she dipped her head instead, and lightly pressed her lips to his scarred chest.

'What are you doing?' he said, recoiling from her touch. 'Can't you see how ugly it is?'

'It's horrible,' she agreed. 'But it's just skin.' She touched a hand to his scarred cheek. 'And it's still you.'

He pulled his cheek away, gave an anguished cry. 'Don't.'

'I won't if you don't want me to.'

He pulled the shirt around him and flung himself from the bed and into an adjoining room. She knew she'd made him angry. She gathered her nightgown and pulled it over her head while he was gone, suddenly embarrassed by her nakedness and sorry she'd said anything about his scars. Sorry they were going to end things this way after such a night. But how else could it end? They'd had a one-night affair and now she was leaving. It wasn't as if there was anything to stay for. It wasn't as if she was in love with him.

She stumbled over the last thought. No. Impossible. She would miss his dark, tortured looks. She would dream of this night for ever. But that was all it could be.

He came back in, wearing a robe this time, looking anywhere but at her. 'I should get going,' she said.

'Yes.'

The word sounded as if it had been dragged from him, and if she'd needed any more reason to leave that was it. Clearly the Count wasn't looking to extend their liaison and why should he? Why should she even want him to? Except that it had been the best sex she'd ever experienced. Probably the best sex she ever would.

She slipped from the bed, balling her panties and pulling her robe around her, giving the tie an extra tug. She would become practical Dr Hunter again, and put away the wanton she had been for just one short night.

And then she heard it—the unmistakable thump of the boat engine drawing closer. 'I guess that's my cue. Thank you, Count Volta, for your hospitality.' She was almost at the door when he finally spoke.

'Stay.'

She blinked and turned around, her veins still sizzling, her heart afraid to beat for a moment at his unexpected request, and then resuming with a thump that challenged the sound of the approaching engine. 'What did you just say?'

He crossed the room in rapid strides until he stood before her. 'I said stay.'

'Why?'

'Because there is no reason to cut and run. People expect you to be here a week. Why do you need to go before you have finished your research?'

He managed to smile a little then, as he touched his fingertips to her forehead and traced down the line of her hair. 'You enjoyed our night together?'

She blushed so hard there was no need to answer. She leaned her face into his touch. 'I thought you were angry with me.'

His fingers stilled at her cheek, his smile vanquished. 'Nobody has ever touched my scars by choice. Yet you put your lips to them. I was—' He looked down at her and she could see both the anguish and the confusion in his eyes. 'Don't you understand? I was shocked.'

She smiled uncertainly up at him, touched by his simple declaration. 'It's not something I generally do, I admit.'

'Then why this time?'

'I don't know. It just seemed the right thing to do.'

'So stay,' he urged, winding his fingers in her hair, pulling her closer. 'That is also the right thing to do. I know it.'

'But the boat...'

He kissed her forehead, then rested his head against hers. 'The boat will return when you need to go. Stay for now and do your work, and when you are finished the boat will come back and you can leave.'

But will I want to?

If she was having trouble leaving now, if she was tempted to stay now, what would it be like in two or three or however many days' time? How could she just board a boat and sail away, knowing she would never see him again?

His hands trailed down her back, tracing the curve of her behind and warming her, firing up desires she'd thought well quenched during the night but which were clearly all too ready to be reignited. What would cool, calm Dr Hunter do? she wondered as he pulled her closer until she could feel the press of his erection against her belly. The wanton in her knew the decision she would make. It made sense to continue her study here, where the documents had been found, and she could do her work during the day and enjoy the pleasures of the night.

It made perfect sense.

Just a few days, she told herself as his mouth dropped to hers, coaxing her lips open with a kiss that promised paradise. She knew it didn't. She knew she was kidding herself. But after all, she rationalised, she had to work *somewhere*.

Three more days she stayed, working on her report during the days, making love with the Count late into the nights.

Three more days that took her closer and closer to the time she knew she would have to leave.

Neither of them spoke of her departure, and she wondered if he'd even noticed—whereas she was counting down the hours, her inevitable departure like a dark cloud growing ever more heavy over her. A dark cloud to replace those that had graced her first two nights here. For now the weather steadily improved, the storms almost forgotten as they made love on crisp moonlit sheets.

But she would have to leave. Her report was almost complete. She was already spinning out the topics, taking more time to check and double-check every word, every reference, avoiding the page on the fatal affliction as much as she dared. Its message was still unsettling.

There was no real reason she should stay.

Except that she could not bring herself to leave.

For with every passing day she knew it would almost kill her to leave—just to walk away and never see Alessandro again, never to feel his strong arms around her, never again to feel the thrust of his hard length. And so she put aside concerns about how long she was taking and how much she wasn't doing and revelled in what he could give her. That was the now. And she had no intention of leaving before she had to.

They were in the bath, breathless and replete, when the phone call came—an urgent call for Dr Hunter from Professor Rousseau, otherwise Bruno would never have bothered them, he assured the Count.

She wrapped herself in a thick robe to take the call, still shuddering from her latest climax and guilty with it, as if the Professor might know, just by talking with her, what she'd so recently been doing.

'Professor,' she said. 'How is your mother?'

'No better, sadly, but no worse. But, tell me, what have you found?'

Grace summarised her findings, unable to keep the excitement from her voice.

'Excellent,' the Professor said. 'Because I have yet another favour to ask you...'

She listened to her colleague's request, one part of her alive to the opportunity she had just been offered, another part so heavy she thought her heart might fall clean out of her chest. But in the end, despite the warring inside her, she knew she had no choice. This was what she had wanted, what she had worked and hoped for.

'Of course, Professor. Of course I will do it.'

'What did she want?' Alessandro asked when he joined her from the bathroom.

'Her mother is still gravely ill. But she has a speaking engagement in London tomorrow evening and there is no way she will make it. She wants me to take her lecture, to use the chance to announce the discovery of the lost pages.'

'And you said yes?'

'Of course I said yes. What else was I supposed to say?' And immediately she felt contrite, because she hadn't wavered, and she'd made it sound as if she couldn't wait to get away. But it hadn't been like that.

'Alessandro,' she reasoned, when he turned away to his dressing room, 'I was always going to leave soon. We both know that.'

'Yes,' he said, glancing back over his shoulder. 'And it's the opportunity you wanted when you took this job. You will be famous the world over, Dr Hunter. People will fill auditoriums and hang onto your every word and credit you for bringing to light an unknown chapter in the development of human society. That's what you wanted all along, isn't it?'

Yes, but why did he have to make it sound as if there was something wrong with that? And why the sudden 'Dr Hunter'? How long had it been since he'd called her that?

'You know what this means to me,' she argued. 'It's my career.'

'Then go,' he flung over his shoulder. 'As you say, we knew you would leave. I'm not stopping you.'

His rapid change of face did not deter her. He'd been disappointed with the news of her imminent departure, she was sure. Or at least unhappy with the news.

'Come with me,' she said on impulse, following him. That way she could have her career and not lose Alessandro. And suddenly not losing Alessandro was more important than she could fathom. 'This is your discovery as much as mine. People will want to know everything they can about the pages.'

'And what could I tell anyone beyond the fact they were found in the caves below my castle? You do not need me there for that.'

'Then come anyway. Come and keep me company. It will do you good to get away from here for a while.'

'My place is here!'

'Why? So you can bury yourself on this island while your castle crumbles around you? Until you end up as dried and broken-down as that fountain outside?'

'You do not know what it is like.'

'Because you're scarred? No, I don't know what it's like to be scarred. I don't know what it's like to have people turn from me in horror. But I do know you can't let your scars define you. You are more than that. And I know I couldn't live that way, burying myself away where nobody might see me.'

'How do you know? You do not know the first thing about me! You have no concept of what it is to like be the only survivor of a party of eighteen. All of them dead. *Dead*! All of them. Apart from me. How do you think that feels? Special? No, Dr Hunter, it does not. Instead it makes me feel damned. Cursed. And the scars are a constant reminder. The scars never let me forget it.'

She felt his pain in the wave of anguish that rolled off him.

'I'm sorry for what happened. I'm sorry for what you suffered—'

He rounded on her. 'You have no concept of what I suffered!'

She recoiled from his outburst. Recoiled and then reloaded, knowing she had to let him know she understood. That she cared. 'I know you lost your fiancée and your friends.'

'I lost much more than that. I lost hope that night. I lost trust.'

Her heart went out to him. 'I understand how that could happen after an accident like that.'

'Do you? I doubt it.' His mouth pulled into a snarl. 'I doubt that you have any idea of the kind of woman my fiancée was—the kind of woman who was so in love with the media fantasy that we were the "It" couple that she would have done anything to maintain it, even when it was already over.

'She threatened to leave me that night, for another of my friends she said wanted her. She would go with him if I did not marry her immediately and fulfil the destiny she had planned. But our relationship was already soured, and her attempt to make me jealous was her last-ditch effort to save our floundering relationship. I told her it was over. And that instead of having a blazing row in a nightclub we would break amicably and put out a joint press release the following day. That night, on our way back to the castle, the accident happened.'

He dragged in air, as if struggling with the memories. 'Someone there overheard us talking and reported it to the police, and so when they came to the hospital, while I was barely recovering from injuries so horrific they expected me to die, it was to inform me that I was the suspect in a mass murder case.'

Ice-cold water sluiced through her veins. She took a step closer. His pain was so clear on his face she could read his story there, etched in his scars. That anyone had suffered so much pain, that *he* had suffered so much, destroyed her. His pain became hers, and she wanted to do anything she could to make things right. Knowing she never could, no matter what she felt for him, knowing now she'd had a right to be scared of staying.

'Alessandro...'

'Can you blame me for burying myself here and hiding away from the media's macabre pursuit, Dr Hunter? Can you begin to understand?'

'It doesn't have to be like that,' she offered softly, but knew it could indeed be like that. 'It never has to be like that again.'

'No. Not if I stay here.'

And she knew she had to play her final card—the final truth she had taken this long to admit. 'And if I told you that I loved you?'

He looked at her then, savagery mixed with tragedy. 'Then I would say you are the most cursed of all.'

CHAPTER TEN

THE applause rang out loud and long in the Washington auditorium, and Dr Grace Hunter smiled in her sensible suit and bowed one final time to the audience, finally able to withdraw to the quiet of the room generously labelled her dressing room—little more than a closet to store her things, really, but at least it provided her with a bolthole.

The lecture in London three months ago had been such a resounding success that she'd been booked almost solid ever since. City after city wanted to hear the story of the lost pages, wanted to see her presentation and hear the lost messages from the fabled book of healing.

She felt a fraud every time—tonight more than ever. How could it be a book of healing, she wondered, when she felt so heartsick every minute of every day? And yet she had the fame she had sought. She had the respect of her peers and her colleagues. She had a book deal and offers of chairs at universities all around the world. Even, in her latest coup, a last-minute slot on a prime time chat show.

How was it possible, with all that success, to feel so wretched?

Or had Alessandro been right? Was she the most cursed of all, loving a man who could not return her love?

She peeled the jacket from her shoulders and pulled the court shoes from her feet, remembering another outfit—a waterfall of silk atop silver sandals that shimmered with every step. His fiancée's dress. Had he realised how much he'd hurt her when she'd heard that? Or hadn't he cared because in his mind she'd already ceased being his fiancée before she had died? Whatever, she supposed she should be thankful that at least he'd taken the trouble to find her something that had never been worn. And it had been a beautiful dress.

She sighed, picking up her programme folder to remind herself of where she would be next. There was no point focusing on the past. She must look to the future. She had career decisions to make and continents to decide between.

There was a knock on the door and she pushed herself from her chair reluctantly, remembering the drinks organised for after her presentation. No doubt a reminder call. She was probably already late.

She pulled open the door, ready to make her excuses, but the words dried up in her throat, incinerated by the lightning bolt that coursed through her. She blinked up at him, her eyes moving past his beauty and his horror to drink in the man himself.

'I heard your lecture,' he told her, when he clearly realised she was incapable of speech. 'You were amazing.'

She swallowed. 'You heard it?'

'I wouldn't have missed it for the world.' And then, perhaps because he sensed she was incapable of rational thought, 'Perhaps you might invite me in?'

And she shook her head to scatter her woolly thoughts and remembered her manners. 'Please, Count Volta.'

'Alessandro,' he corrected, and her stunned heart—not yet ready to hope—warmed just a little.

There was barely room for the two of them. He refused to sit, his wide frame shrinking what little space there was. 'What's happened?' she asked, knowing what it must have cost him to leave the castle—knowing what it must have cost him in the stares and whispers of strangers, in the camera flashes of the paparazzi. 'Why are you here? Someone will have seen you.'

His tortured eyes confirmed it, but he shook his head, as if dispensing with that mentality. 'You once said to me that I should not define myself by my scars—'

'No—please. I had no right. I had no idea of what had really happened.'

'Grace,' he said, taking one of her hands in his own, 'you had every right. You were right.' He took a breath, and then another, and she could see how much it was costing him to tell her this. 'Don't you see? I became my scars. I hid behind them because it was easier to live in the dark. Because it was easier than facing the light.'

'It's okay,' she said, wanting to spare him any more pain, knowing what it must have cost him in media attention to get here, suspecting there was a pack of photographers waiting outside right now to see him. 'You don't have to explain it to me.'

'But I do. Don't you see, Grace?' He took hold of her other hand, held them both up in his. 'You brought me back the light. You were the one who chased the darkness away. You made me see it was all right to live again.'

Her heart skipped a beat, and then another, because she didn't want to believe what it might possibly mean. 'I did?'

He smiled. 'You did. You turned up in my dark world and showed me what life could be like with your enthusiasm, with your joy of discovery. At first, I admit, I hated you for it, because you reminded me of all the things I had lost and of all the things I would never know again. But bit by bit I wanted to be part of it. I wanted to share your light. I wanted to share your joy.'

She thought back to the disastrous dinner and his cruel comment about the dress. 'You were protecting yourself.'

'I couldn't let myself crumble. It took me years to recover after the accident. I couldn't let anything like that happen again, even if it meant losing the best thing that had ever happened to me. I was desperate to find some kind of outlet. I hadn't played the piano for ten years until you came. It was something I associated with *her*. It was part of my former life and I couldn't bring myself to touch the keyboard until wanting you drove me to it. Drove me back to something I loved. Just as you drove me back to life and living and I realised it didn't have to be the same.'

Tears leaked from her eyes. Her heart was pounding in her chest.

'You kissed my scars, Grace. I was shocked and I overreacted, but do you have any idea what was happening to me? You broke something free inside me, something dark and poisoned and toxic. And bit by bit you chased the blackness away.'

For the first time she noticed the moisture glazing his eyes too, as he brought her hands up to his mouth, closed his eyes and kissed them.

'I had to come,' he said at last. 'I knew it from the first day you left. I knew I had missed an opportunity so golden that it might never come again. But still I couldn't do it. I told myself you were busy becoming famous, that you could not possibly have any place for me in your life. Fear bound me to the castle, just as you said. But as the days and weeks went on I had to know. I had to find out for myself, whatever it took.'

He hesitated then, as if searching the depths of his soul for words. 'Grace, you once told me you loved me. Is there any chance you might love me again? Love a man who was too blind to recognise his own love when it stared him in the face?'

Her heart swelled so large with his words she thought it might explode with happiness. She threw herself into his arms, drinking in his scent, relishing the hard plane of his chest. 'I will always love you, Alessandro. *Always.*'

And he sighed, almost with relief, as if there had ever been any doubt, and drew her closer into his embrace. 'You do not know how I have longed to hear those words again—if only for the opportunity to tell you that I love you with everything this scarred heart can offer. You have it all. But I know you have your career, and that must come first—'

Alarm bells sounded. 'What do you mean that must come first? Before what?'

'We can work it out. You will prefer to continue working, of course. You will not want to be tied down...'

'Alessandro, what are you saying? Maybe you should spell it out first.'

His dark eyes were troubled and uncertain, and she had never seen him so vulnerable. He had risked everything for her today, she realised. Everything. And she would love him for what that had cost him for ever.

'You have your work.'

'Tell me!'

'I hoped—I wondered—so long as it doesn't interfere with your work—' she glared at him '—I wondered if you might agree to become my wife?'

'Yes!' she cried, tears of joy springing to her eyes. 'Yes, I will marry you, Alessandro. Yes, I will become your wife.'

And his face lit up brighter than she had ever seen it, until both sides of his face were beautiful, both sides of him magically, wonderfully hers.

EPILOGUE

THE dock had been sanded and oiled till it gleamed in the sun, the rocks bordering the track freshly painted white. Flags fluttered gaily along the route, and the small harbour was filled with dozens of bobbing white pleasure craft.

It was to be a small affair, he'd promised her. No more than two or three hundred guests. And under the lure of a perfect summer's day they spilled out of the massive ballroom and filled the grounds around the castle, admiring the view across the sea to the Italian coast or having their pictures taken in front of the dolphin fountain, where the water played and splashed like jewels in the bright sunshine.

He looked magnificent, she thought as she caught a glimpse of him through the crowd, in one of his beautifully tailored suits that showed the long, lean line of his body to perfection. He looked magnificent and at ease with himself at last—as if he'd cast his demons from his shoulders, as if he'd come to terms with his past. He'd even wooed the inevitable media, so it was now fully behind him, and covering his wedding as if it was some kind of fairytale. And it *was* a fairytale, she knew.

But it was much more than that. *He* was much more than that. Right now he was talking to someone hidden by the crowd, his beautiful scarred face animated and alive.

He caught her eye across the space and held it, and she felt that now familiar slow burn of heat flare up inside her as he excused himself and headed her way, looking neither left nor right as he cut a swathe towards her. He was at her side a heartbeat later, sweeping her up in one arm and swinging her around.

'Have I told you how beautiful you look today, Countess Volta?'

She smiled. 'Maybe once or twice,' she said, though they both knew it was many, many more times than that. 'And have I told you how magnificent you look, my husband?'

'So many times,' he growled, nuzzling her ear, 'that I fear I may just start to believe it.'

'Believe it,' she said. 'You are the most handsome man here.'

'Grace—'

'No, it is true. You are smiling so much you are like a beacon. Everyone wants to talk to you. Why else has it taken this long to have a moment with you alone?'

'I was just talking to Professor Rousseau.'

Grace looked around, trying to find her through the crowd. 'Oh, I should have come over to you. She doesn't know many people here, Alessandro.'

'She's fine. I left her talking to my best man.'

'To Bruno? I wouldn't have thought they would have much in common.'

'On the contrary. It turns out they both have pirate ancestors. Bruno has offered to show the Professor through the caves below the castle.'

'He has?' She scanned the crowd, which finally parted enough that she could see them both in deep conversation. As if aware he was being discussed, Bruno suddenly looked up and gave a bashful smile. 'He smiled at me,' she said. 'Bruno actually smiled.'

The man beside her laughed, and she found so much joy in the sound that she wondered... 'Do you think it's true, Alessandro—the legend of the *Salus Totus*? Do you think it really is a book of healing? Do you think it a coincidence that it was found here?'

He took her hands in his own. 'I think you are the healer here, Grace. You came to an island where a monster resided, where only darkness existed. You lit up that world and shook it until your light and your love chased the darkness and the monster away. And I will love you for it for ever.'

He kissed her as tears sprang to her eyes. Tears of love. Tears of joy. Tears for the wasted years, and tears for all the years that were yet to come.

Years they would spend together.

* * * * *

THE RELUCTANT QUEEN
Caitlin Crews

CHAPTER ONE

"HELLO, Princess."

It was a dark voice, low and deep, and echoed hard and deep in Lara Canon's bones—making them sing out in recognition. She turned without conscious thought, as if compelled, searching for the man responsible, though some part of her knew at once who he must be. Her gaze flicked across the parking lot of the unremarkable supermarket in her Denver, Colorado, neighborhood, scanning out from the side of her car where she'd stopped still.

She found him at once, unerringly, as if he'd commanded it. Her heart began to beat wildly, even as her skin prickled.

He was even more compelling than his voice, tall and broad like a warrior, with jet-black hair and deep gray eyes above a hard, unsmiling mouth. He held himself with an ease she knew at once was deceptive—he was too watchful, too ready. He wore a black, tight shirt that strained against the tautly packed muscles of his broad chest and flat abdomen, and trousers in the same color that clung to powerful legs and lean hips. He was beautiful in the way that dangerous thunderstorms were beautiful, and Lara discovered that she was breathless.

He was the most gorgeous thing she'd ever seen, for all that he was the most arresting. And more than that, she recognized him. *She knew him.*

She had thought she'd never see him again. She felt her pulse pound beneath her skin.

"I did not expect that you would grow to favor your father," he said, those remote, storm-colored eyes seeming to see right through her, shocking her, looking straight into the past she'd long denied. The shopping bag in her arms slipped a few inches as her fingers lost feeling. As panic surged through her.

She realized two things, clutching at the brown paper bag before it fell to the asphalt at her feet. First, that he was not speaking English. And second, that she could understand the language he *was* speaking.

It made her think at once, of course, of Alakkul. Her father's tiny, oft-contested country in the Eurasian, sometime-Soviet mountains, where his family had ruled with iron fists and an inflated sense of their own consequence for generations.

The country she and her mother had escaped from, in the dark of night, when she was sixteen years old. The country that she had been running from, in one way or another, ever since. And the last place she had seen this man, when he had still been more of a boy. When he had been far less beautiful, far less dangerous, and had still managed to break her teenaged heart.

Her stomach clenched into a thick, tight knot. She told herself it was panic—that it could not be that old, familiar desire she'd been so overwhelmed by as a girl. They were in a busy parking lot, filled with people on this bright June evening. He was standing far enough away that she didn't think he could reach over and grab her—and anyway, she was twenty-eight years old. Her father could hardly attempt to regain custody *now*. There was no reason for him to be here. And therefore no reason for her to acknowledge their shared history.

"I'm sorry," she said. In English. She shrugged to indicate her lack of comprehension and, hopefully, polite disinterest.

It had been so long. Maybe she was seeing ghosts. Maybe it wasn't him at all. "Can I help you with something?"

He smiled, and it was far more disturbing than his voice, or his hard, shocking beauty. It made his gray eyes warm slightly, with a flash of what looked like sympathy. It confused Lara even as it set off a tiny trail of flickering flames across her skin, licking up and down her limbs. Reminding her. Making her yearn for things she dared not name.

"You are the only one who can help me," he said, in his perfect, exotically accented English. His mouth crooked. "You must marry me. As you promised to do twelve years ago."

She laughed, of course. What else could she do? She laughed, even as old memories chased through her head— long-buried images of crystal-clear mountain lakes, snow-capped peaks jutting in the distance, the spires of an ancient castle hewn from the very rock of the steep hills. A lean, feral young man with dark gray eyes, looking down at her with a fierce expression while her heart beat too fast and the white-cloaked priests murmured archaic, improbable words through the haze of incense and ritual. His head bent close to hers to whisper secrets in the middle of a great festival dinner, making her shiver. His smile, his occasional laughter, that fire in his stormy eyes when he gazed at her…

How long had she told herself those images were part of a dream? That they could not be anything *but* a dream? Yet the man who stood before her was undeniably, inarguably real.

And worse, she knew him. Her body knew him—and was reacting exactly as it had then, when she had been so young. She'd spent a long time convincing herself that all that fire had been no more than a young girl's fantasy. That he could not possibly do these things to her. That she had embellished, exaggerated, as young girls did.

"Thank you for the offer," she said, as if she was placating him. As if she did not, in fact, remember him. "But I'm afraid I have a personal policy against marrying strange men who approach me in parking lots."

"I am Adel Qaderi," he said, in that calm yet implacable voice, his gray eyes on hers, that name sounding within her like a gong. Her breath tangled in her throat. "I am no stranger to you. I am your betrothed, as you know very well."

It was such an odd, old word. Lara concentrated on that—pushing away the fluttering of her pulse, the constriction in her throat. The onslaught of too many memories she'd thought forgotten long ago.

"I'm sorry," she said, dismissing him. If she didn't accept this was happening, it didn't have to happen, did it? "I'm late for a—"

"You are the Crown Princess of Alakkul," Adel said in that low, commanding voice, somehow making it impossible for Lara to turn and get into her car as she knew she should. "The last of an ancient bloodline, warriors and kings throughout history. The only child of the great King Azat, may he rest in peace."

She felt the blood drain from her face. Her knees wobbled beneath her.

"May he…?" she echoed. She shook her head, trying to clear it. What could this mean? How could it be true? Her father was the monster under her bed, the nightmare that lay in wait when she closed her eyes. Hadn't her mother always told her so? "He's…*dead*?"

"At least you do not deny your own father," Adel said, his expression stern. He moved closer to her but then stopped, as if he felt called to an action he chose not to take. Still, somehow, she knew he grieved for her father in all the ways she could not. It made a headache bloom to life in her temples. "Perhaps we can dispense with the rest of this game of pretend now."

"You approached me in a parking lot, like a vagrant," Lara hissed. Unwilling to face what he'd just told her. Unwilling to imagine what it might mean. "What did you think my re-action would be?"

"I did so deliberately." His gaze was cool. Assessing. *Dangerous.* "I assumed you would feel more at ease in a public place. After all, you have spent most of your life running away at the slightest hint of your homeland."

Lara shifted the bag in her arms, and wished her head would stop spinning. How was she supposed to act? Feel? She had not heard from her autocratic father directly in twelve years. She had not wanted to hear from him. If asked even five minutes before, she would have announced without a qualm that she hated the man.

But that did not mean she'd wanted him dead.

"I need to inform my mother…" she began, her temples pounding, wondering how fragile, prone-to-hysteria Marlena would be likely to take such news. Wondering, too, what her mother would center her life around now there was no more King Azat to hate and fear and blame. But perhaps that was unkind.

"Your mother is being notified even now," Adel replied coolly.

Lara found herself staring at the play of muscle in his strong arms, his hard abdomen. She felt her body's treacherous heat, its instant response to the very sight of him, despite her emotions.

"I am afraid your business is with me, Princess. I cannot allow you the necessary time to grieve." Was his tone ironic? Or did she only imagine his judgment? Was that guilt she felt, pooling inside of her? "We must wed immediately."

"You are insane," she told him, when she could speak. When the red haze of confusion and emotion receded slightly. When she could jerk her attention away from his warrior's body. "You cannot really believe I'll marry you!"

Adel smiled again, though this time, there was nothing particularly sympathetic about it. Where was that younger man she remembered, who had been so eager to see her smile?

"I understand that this is a shock," he said. "But let me be clear. You have only two possible choices before you, and while I am aware neither one is necessarily easy, you must choose one of them."

"Your attempt at compassion is insulting," Lara managed to say, her hands clenched tight into the bag she held. Part of her wanted to fling the sack at him as he stood near the trunk of her sensible sedan. And then run. Only the fact that he probably expected that reaction kept her from it.

"Nonetheless, it is real," he said. His storm-colored eyes moved to hers, and darkened. "It would never have been my choice to confront you in this way, with this news. I regret the necessity. But it does not change anything."

"I have no idea what you're talking about," Lara said after a moment, her temper kicking in—replacing the wild swirl of far trickier feelings. Anger was better. Anger *felt* better—more productive. "And more important? I don't care."

"Yet you must listen," he told her. So quiet. So sure. And she could only stare at him. And obey. "I am sorry for that, too, but so it is."

There was something about the way he looked at her then that…bothered her, in a way she couldn't quite categorize. As if he could see the buried truths she'd denied existed for years. The old dreams. The yearnings for a life, a family, the kind of things other girls took for granted while she trailed around after Marlena, cleaning up her messes. The way she'd felt about him all those years ago, the things she'd dreamed they'd do together—

Lara blinked, and steeled herself against him—and the surprising swell of something like grief that she would have sworn she'd never feel.

"What, then?" she asked, her voice too rough, as she fought

back the unwieldy emotions that shifted and rolled within her. "What is it you think I need to hear?"

"You have a choice to make," he said again, and the worst part, Lara realized in a sort of horror, was that his voice was kind, his eyes the same. As if he understood exactly what she was going through—as if he *knew*.

And yet he was continuing anyway, wasn't he? He was an Alakkulian male. An Alakkulian king. Just like her father, he thought only of himself. That much was blatantly obvious, no matter how kind his eyes might seem. No matter her memories of his smile, of his tenderness.

"The only choice I will be making," she told him, enunciating clearly, deliberately, with razor-sharp precision, as if sounding tough would make her feel that way, too, "is to get in my car and drive away from here. From you. From this ridiculous conversation. I suggest you get out of the way, unless you'd like me to run you over."

"You did not merely promise to marry me, as any young girl might," Adel said in the same calm, commanding tone, as if she had not just threatened him. "You entered into a binding legal contract."

"I was a teenager," Lara retorted. "No court in the world would ever hold me to it. It's absurd you would think otherwise—this is not the Stone Age!"

"You overestimate the progressive nature of the world's courts, I think," he replied, something almost like humor flashing briefly across his face. But she did not want to think of him as human, as capable of humor as he'd been before, and ignored it. "But in any case, it does not matter. Your father signed for you when you were too young, as is the custom. When you came of age you did not withdraw your consent from the contract—which, according to the laws of Alakkul, means you thus agreed that you entered into the terms of the contract of your own free will."

"I will not marry you," she said. Her shoulders tightened, her chin rose like a fighter's. "I would rather die."

"There is no need for such theater," Adel replied in a faintly reproving tone. Yet his mouth curved slightly—as if he found her amusing. It made her temper kick in again. That, she told herself, was the feeling that pounded through her, shaking her. "You may break the contract, if that is your wish. But there is a price."

"Let me guess." Lara scraped her heavy curls back from her face with an impatient jerk of her hand. "My honor will be smeared? My family name forever muddied? Isn't that how you people think?"

"By 'you people,'" he asked, his voice staying even though a cold fire blazed to life in his gaze, "am I to understand you mean your own people? Your countrymen?"

"I'll live with the dishonor," Lara told him, not wanting to admit the twist of shame she felt move through her. Much less the odd urge she had to reach over and touch him. "Quite happily."

"As you wish," Adel said with that great calm that, for some reason, infuriated her as surely as if he'd openly taunted her. It made her want to scratch at him, poke at him—made her want to see beneath the surface, rip off the mask she was sure he wore, see what lurked beneath. She just wanted to *touch* him.

She had no idea where that urge came from. Nor why it seemed to move through her like a scalding heat, rippling over her skin and pooling in places it shouldn't.

The city seemed to mute itself around them, the parking lot fading, the bright sky above and the slight breeze from the Rocky Mountains in the distance disappearing. There was only this dangerous, compelling warrior of a man in place of the boy she had once known, and too many emotions to name. She felt...pulled to him. Drawn. As if he'd cast a spell with that fascinating mouth and that commanding, resolute gaze of his, and she was helpless to resist, no matter how many reasons she had to avoid him and how little she wanted to hear what he might have to say.

But if there was one thing she refused to be, it was helpless.

"Wonderful," she said, pulling herself back from the brink of disaster. Her tone was acerbic, as much to defend herself against this man as to convince herself he was not getting to her in so many odd, uncomfortable ways. "I'm glad you traveled across the world to tell me all of this. You can consider our absurd betrothal ended."

"As you wish," he said again. But he did not move. His gaze seemed to sharpen, as if he was some great predator and she nothing but prey. She fought off an involuntary shiver. "You need only pay me the bride price."

"The bride price?" she repeated, caught as much by the sudden ferocity in his dark gaze as by the words themselves.

"Your dowry was the throne of Alakkul, Princess," Adel said quietly, deliberately. "I am afraid that the sum my family paid for you was significant, give or take such things as the exchange rate, the rate of inflation, and so on."

He named a number that she could not possibly have heard right—a number so astronomically high that it, too, made her laugh. It was as patently absurd as him suddenly appearing in a parking lot and announcing he was going to marry her, just as she'd dreamed when she'd first left Alakkul—and as impossible.

"I have nothing even approaching that amount of money, and never will," she said flatly. "I am an accountant. I live an entirely normal and ordinary life. That amount of money is a fantasy."

"Not to the Queen of Alakkul," he said, and something flared between them, hot and bright, making her breath tangle in her throat, making her ache low in her belly. "Or to me."

"That is another fantasy, one I have no interest in."

"I am a compassionate man," Adel said after a moment, though the expression he wore made her doubt it. "I will release you from your obligations to me, if that is your desire. You need only repay what your mother stole from the palace when she disappeared twelve years ago. It is not so much. A mere nine hundred thousand dollars, and some precious jewels."

"Nine hundred thousand dollars," Lara repeated in disbelief. "You must be joking. I don't have it—and if my mother took it, it is no more than she deserved, after what my father subjected her to!"

Adel merely inclined his head. "I will not argue with you about your mother," he said. "Nor will I debate your choices with you. They are simple. Marry me, or pay the price."

He held up an autocratic hand when she started to speak, and she knew deep in her bones that he was every inch a king as well as a warrior. She should hate that—him. And yet her treacherous body, instead of finding him repulsive, *yearned*.

"There is not much time, Princess," he said. "I regret the necessity, but you must make your decision. Now."

CHAPTER TWO

HE APPROVED of the woman she'd become, Adel thought, her fierceness and her attempts at fearlessness, and was not certain why that surprised him.

"Do you accept credit cards?" she asked icily after a moment, her silver-blue eyes glittering in the late-afternoon light, even as she held herself so rigidly, so determinedly still. "If so, I am certain we can work something out."

Adel only smiled, enjoying her, even under these circumstances. The girl he had never forgotten for a moment had become a woman he wanted to know better. "You are stalling."

"Of course I am." She shifted her weight and let the paper sack she carried fall to the ground at her feet. He heard the faint crunch of glass against the pavement, but she only glared at him. "It will take me more than thirty seconds to choose between marriage to a man I hardly know or a lifetime in debt I'll never pay off. The interest rates alone would kill me! You'll just have to wait."

He liked that, too. She was as much the child of the late King Azat, his revered mentor, as she was of the faithless woman who was her mother. Brave. Vibrant. And she would be his wife. His queen, as had been decided so many years ago. The warrior in him appreciated the way she stood so straight, emotion darkening her eyes but not overtaking her, her body lean and supple and strong. The king in him imagined the future her blood assured, the children they would bear together, the way they would rule his beloved Alakkul. And the man in him wanted to taste the fullness of her mouth, and sink his fingers into the dark glossy waves of her long hair.

Just as he'd always wanted her, even back when they were both young.

He had wanted her even after her lying mother had spirited her away, taking her far from her home—far from Adel. He had wanted her in all the years in between, when the old King insisted they leave her to her new life and Adel had wondered when he could ever lay claim to the woman who had always been his. He wanted her as she denied him, as she fought with him, as she looked at him as if he was her enemy.

He had wanted her so long, it had become as much a part of him as his own name. It did not matter what she'd done in all the intervening years. It did not even matter if she'd forgotten him. He was here now, and she was his.

She was far too Western. She was dressed for summer in America—all bare skin and tight clothes that outlined curves his hands itched to touch. Her hair was untamed, uncovered, a silken black mass of curls spilling around her creamy shoulders. Her high, full breasts filled out the tight, V-necked shirt she wore to perfection, while her slim hips and long legs were encased in scandalously tight denim. Her feet were bare to his sight, her polished pink toenails in thonged sandals.

These things should have displeased him. Perhaps even angered him. Yet they did not. She did not.

At all.

He was fascinated.

"Explain this to me," she said after a moment, her eyes meeting his and then falling, as if she could sense the direction of his thoughts. "My father signed me away to you?

When I was twelve? And you are the sort of man who wants to honor that kind of archaic, misogynistic agreement?"

"Your father was the King of Alakkul," Adel said swiftly, not rising to the obvious bait. "And I am his chosen successor. You are his only daughter, and the last of your bloodline. It is fitting that you become my queen."

It was more than fitting—it was necessary, though he did not plan to share that with her. Not now. Not yet.

Her throat worked. Her eyes clouded over, though with temper or hurt, he could not tell. "How romantic," she managed to say.

"Surely you have always known this day would come, Princess," he replied, keeping his voice even, wondering why he felt the urge to comfort her. There was no point addressing that bitter note in her voice. "You have been permitted to live freely for years. But it was always on borrowed time."

"Interestingly, I was under the impression that I was simply living my life," she said, her gaze freezing into a glare. "I had no idea you were lying in wait!"

"You cannot tell me you do not remember me." He saw the tell-tale brush of color on her cheeks, heard the catch of her breath. He remembered the sweet taste of their first, stolen kiss. The music of her sigh of pleasure when he touched her. He could see she did, too. "I can see that you do."

"It might as well be a dream!" she said fiercely, though her flushed cheeks told a different tale. "That's what I thought it was!"

"Life is often unfair, Princess," he said, his voice low, his attention on the way she stood on the balls of her feet, as if she meant to run. Would she dare? "But that does not change the facts of things."

"There are your facts, and then there are my facts," she said in a low voice. She took a breath, and her silver-blue eyes turned to steel. He liked that, too. The warrior in him, who had fought and trained and gladly suffered to achieve all that he had done, sang his approval. "You can go ahead and sue me for your money. I won't pay it. And whatever the courts in your tiny little country might say, the court of public opinion will have only one word for a king who chases down a defenseless woman like this. *Bully.*"

Adel smiled then, because she was so much more than he had dared imagine, when he'd thought of her growing up so far from her people, her traditions, him. She was not her mother's daughter at all, as he had feared, no matter how that worthless woman had tried to poison her against all that was hers.

"You will make a magnificent queen," he told her, though he doubted she wished to hear such things. "It is your birthright."

She shook her head, as if he'd insulted her, and turned her back on him. It was a deliberate dismissal. And yet he felt it like a caress, shooting through him, desire and admiration coursing through his veins. *Finally,* something in him whispered. *A woman who is worthy. A woman who is not afraid.*

"Find another queen," she threw back over her shoulder as she opened her car door. "I'm not interested in the job."

Adel moved closer, putting out his hand to hold the door of her car open as she went to get in. He did not crowd her—but he also did not step back when she whipped back around to face him. He stood there for a moment, waiting until her breath came faster, and her gaze dropped to his mouth. He could feel the tension wind between them, and longed to close the distance between them—longed to take her mouth with his and reintroduce himself in the best way he could.

"I spoke of facts, Princess," he said, when she dragged her gaze back to his. "Let me share a few with you. I have every intention of marrying you, as we both swore to do in our betrothal ceremony twelve years ago. That is a fact."

"Your intentions are your business," she replied calmly,

though her eyes flashed blue steel. "They have nothing to do with me."

"If you do not honor your obligations," he continued as if she had not spoken, "I will not simply be forced to take measures to secure the bride price owed to me. I will also have no choice but to have your deceitful mother arrested and returned to Alakkul, where her theft of so much money and so many jewels—not to mention her kidnapping of the Crown Princess—will no doubt result in an extremely long and unpleasant jail term. If not death. As your husband and your king, of course, I would be willing to forgive such criminal acts on the part of your relative. But why would I extend such a courtesy to a stranger?"

"And again," she said after a long moment, her mouth trembling slightly, as if he'd hurt her. "What words do you think come to mind when you say such things?"

"I cannot compromise," he said softly. Fiercely. "I will not."

"And that is what kind of man you've grown into," she replied in the same voice, as something like an ache, a need, swelled in the warm summer air between them. Adel wanted to touch it. Her. "So much for the boy who promised he would never hurt me, that he would lay down his life to avoid it."

He wanted to smile—did she not realize how much she revealed with that memory? How much room she gave him to hope? But he refrained.

"I wish I could place your feelings above all else," he said, inclining his head slightly. "But that is not who I am. I cannot pretend that I will not do anything and everything in my power to secure you. And thus the throne. I owe nothing less to the people of Alakkul." He moved slightly, closer, unable to keep his distance as he should. She was too much—too magnetic, too proud. Too…everything he'd dreamed. "*Your* people, Princess."

"You can call me *Princess* all you like," she said, strong

emotion cracking across her face, in her voice. "That doesn't make it so. I left all of that behind. I have no interest in a foreign country I can hardly remember."

"What will spark your interest, I wonder?" he asked, hearing the danger in his own voice, even as he saw her awareness of it, of him, in her gaze. "Are you as cold-hearted as you would like me to believe? Are you prepared for the consequences of your refusal? Not just to your faithless mother," he said coldly when she began to speak, "but to the very people you claim to care nothing about. If you do not take the throne with me, I will have to fight for it. That is not a euphemism. I am talking about civil war."

She rocked back on her feet, and dragged in a deep, ragged breath. Her eyes were unreadable when they met his again, dark gray now instead of blue.

"Why ask me at all?" she demanded, her voice strained. "Why pretend that I have a choice to make if I do not?"

He wanted to trace the shape of her delicate cheekbones, the bold line of her nose, the full swell of her lips. He did not understand what he felt then—tenderness? Affection? Need? All of the above at once?

"Here is what I will promise you," he said abruptly, called somehow to fix the darkness of her expression. "I will honor you and respect you, a claim I do not make to many without cause, but one I made to you twelve years ago. I will not take lightly the sacrifice you are making today. I doubt I am an easy man, but I will try to be fair."

He saw tears at the back of her eyes, making them shine too bright. But she did not let them fall. He saw the panic, the uncertainty, the fear. But then she swallowed, and let her hands drop to her sides, and he knew it was as much a surrender as a challenge.

He could handle both. He'd been waiting for her for over a decade. For the whole of his life. He was amazed at how much, how deeply and how completely, he wanted to handle her. In every sense of the term.

"Congratulations," she said bitterly. "You've won yourself a completely unwilling queen."

Adel did not, could not care if she thought she hated him now. He would win her. He had won her years before—and she had already showed him she remembered more than she claimed she did. He would build on those memories, and he would win her all over again. And this time, in the way a man won a woman he meant to keep.

"I will take you any way I can get you," Adel said now, and extended his hand, keeping the hard, bright triumph that flared inside of him under tight control. She was his. Finally. "Come," he said. "Our future awaits."

He saw her pulse go wild in her throat, saw her remarkable eyes widen a fraction. He saw her waver. He saw her legs shake as if she fought against the urge to bolt. Still, he held out his hand, and waited.

She bit her lip, surrendered, and slid her hand into his.

She had no choice.

Everything seemed to burst into speed and color, exploding all around her.

There was the feel of his warm, strong palm, his skin against hers, arrowing deep into her, making her soften and yearn. *Just like before.* There was his strong, dangerous body too close to hers—so close she imagined she could *feel* his heat—and the way she wanted to lean into him even as her mind shrieked in denial of everything that was happening. Her body had already decided. Her body had chosen him years ago, and was now exultant at his return. It was her mind that reeled, that was desperate for an out.

But what was her alternative? Her mother jailed? *War?* How could she possibly live with any of that, knowing she'd had the power to prevent it and had refused?

And she did not doubt that Adel Qaderi was more than capable of the things he'd promised. She could feel his ruthlessness taking her over like an ache in the bones, making it impossible for her to breathe. It was his ruthlessness, she told herself firmly, and nothing more—certainly not that old, demanding heat that only he raised in her. Certainly not that.

Adel raised his hand, and they were suddenly surrounded—by a fleet of hard-mouthed, serious-looking men who spoke in staccato tones into earpieces and herded Lara into a limousine she had not seen idling nearby.

It was only when she was tucked inside the car and it was speeding away, while her head spun wildly, that her eyes fell on the pieces of luggage on the seat opposite her. She recognized them at once. She had last seen them in the hall closet of her apartment.

She stared at them for a moment, her brain refusing to make the obvious and only connection, and then whipped her head around to stare at the man who sat with such devastating confidence beside her.

He only raised his dark brow, and watched her.

He had known she would surrender.

He had planned it.

"Your belongings have been packed up and are being shipped," he said without the slightest hint of apology in his tone. But why should he apologize? He'd won. "But should you wish for anything else, it is yours."

"Except my freedom," she said with more bitterness than she'd intended. "My *life*."

"Except that," he agreed, his voice moving from that exotic steel to a softer velvet.

He shocked her then by reaching over and taking her hand in his far bigger one, holding it between his palms.

Lara jumped, a shudder working through her body, as she stared at the place they were connected, her fingers curling toward his. She felt herself blush, hard, the heat prickling over her and casting her in a hot, breathless red.

"Is it so terrible?" he asked softly, very nearly amused, his voice a caress in the stillness of the car's plush interior. "I am not a bad man."

"You'll understand if I choose to reserve judgment on that," she said in a voice that sounded so much stronger, so much crisper, than she felt—and yet she did not pull her hand away from his. "Given that you are currently blackmailing me into marrying you, as if we are in some gothic novel."

"You intrigue me, Princess," he said, his voice insinuating itself in places it should not have been able to reach. Heat moved between them, or she simply burned, and she could not pretend that she was not at least partly as motivated by that as she was by her concern for the rest of it. What did that make her?

"That sounds like a fantastic basis for a marriage," she managed to say. "You are intrigued, I am forced into it against my will, and the fate of my mother and all the citizens of Alakkul hangs in the balance. How delightful."

"Ah," he said in a voice that made her think of much darker delights, skin against skin, long, hot nights, all those things she'd long imagined with him but thought would never come to pass, "but will is a delicate thing, is it not?"

He lifted her hand to his mouth. Trapped, captivated—*appalled*, she told herself!—she only watched. As he turned her hand in his. As he brought her palm closer to the hard line of his full lips. As his thunderstorm eyes met hers, electric, demanding.

And as he kissed the center of her palm, sending a lightning bolt of impossible desire directly into her core.

CHAPTER THREE

LARA snatched her hand back, jumping in her seat as if he'd bitten her. And then she felt herself melt into a wild heat, imagining what it might be like if he did exactly that.

"What are you doing?" she demanded, horrified at herself, curling the palm he'd tasted into a fist and shoving it into her lap. Would she fall for him so easily, so quickly? After twelve years and far too much water under the bridge? "You can't— you can't *possibly*—"

"We are to be married," he said, leaning back in his seat, his gray eyes gleaming silver now, his hard mouth allowing the smallest curve. "What do you think I'm doing?"

She could not think at all—that was the problem! Her mind was a loud, buzzing blank, like static, and it was all too much to take. Adel's unexpected appearance in the parking lot. The threats, the compulsion. The news of her father, which she could still hardly bear to think about, could still barely bring herself to accept as real. Her own capitulation that had led to her presence in this car. And it was his fault! She could not seem to form a single coherent thought, save that. *He* had done this. Lara was perfectly clear about the fact that Adel Qaderi was capable of anything. It was just as her mother had always said—Alakkulian men could not be trusted.

Hadn't he just proved that? What decent, honorable man

would behave as he had done, under these insane circumstances?

Her own pounding need, her own desire—Lara could not let herself consider.

"How can you possibly imagine that I would welcome your advances?" she hissed at him. "I will never—"

"Never is a very long time," he said, with a soft laugh, as if she delighted him. "Be careful how you use the word. It might come to haunt you."

Suddenly, the future she could not escape yawned open in front of her, a deep, black hole. It was one thing to offer to make a sacrifice, knowing it was the right thing—the only thing—to do. But how was she meant to survive *this*? The day-to-day, moment-to-moment reality of being in this man's possession? Being a wife? A queen? A *lover*, a voice inside whispered, and her stomach clenched again.

"Are you so delusional that you truly believe that a woman in my position would *ever* want you to touch her?" she asked, her voice rasping over everything she could not say, everything she feared—including her own reactions to this man. *Especially* her reactions. The heat between her legs. The ache in her too-heavy breasts. Her inability to draw a full breath. The car seemed too close around her. *He* was too close.

"I don't know about a woman in your position," he murmured, stretching his arm out along the back of the seat and in so doing, drawing her attention away from her own panic and bringing it to his electric physicality. "That is far too abstract for me. I can only tell you what is concrete." His hot gaze dropped from her eyes to her mouth. His voice lowered. "What I see, what I smell, what I know."

"That I can barely remember you?" she supplied in desperation, shifting to be sure she avoided even the faintest brush of contact with his arm. "That I want nothing to do with you?"

"That your body wants me, no matter what you might say

to the contrary," he said, seemingly unperturbed by her acidity. He even smiled, as if he could see the way her breasts firmed, her thighs clenched. As if he knew her treacherous body better than she did. As if he understood the potent, wild combination of emotion and arousal that made Lara feel like a stranger to herself.

"You know nothing about me," she threw out, desperately. "We might as well be complete strangers!"

He leaned forward, and Lara had to force herself not to squeak like a mouse and shrink away from him. But pretending to be strong only left her far too close to him. Close enough to see the faint hint of his beard along his strong jaw. Close enough to find herself mesmerized by that hard mouth she now knew could be devastatingly soft, if he chose. Close enough to smell the faint hint of sandalwood that clung to him, and something else, something male and only his, beneath.

"We are not strangers," he said, his eyes gleaming pure silver now. "We never were. I am the man who will be your husband, your lover, the father of your children. These things will happen, Princess. Perhaps not today. Perhaps not even soon. But believe me, they will happen."

"I said I would marry you," she breathed, locked in his uncompromising gaze, lost in the spell he cast around them. "I can't do anything else, can I?"

"No." His eyes seemed to warm, and to warm her, too. "You cannot do anything else."

"I never said anything about...the rest of it," she continued, deeply unnerved. She was aware of him—every part of him. The way he looked at her, the heat that seemed to emanate from his tautly muscled form, even the places his gaze touched as it swept over her. She had to force herself to breathe. And then again.

His smile deepened, as if she was precious to him some-

how. As if she was more than merely a pawn in his game.
But how could that be?

He reached down with the hand he'd laid against the back
of their seat and traced a line along her jaw, from temple to
lip, until he held her chin in his fingers.

She knew she should jerk away. She told herself hers was
the fascination of the fly for the spider, the moth for the flame,
and it would be suicidal to pay more attention to the unfamiliar heat and *want* that scorched her than to her own mind—

But she did not move.

She only watched him. Helpless. Caught. And unable, in
that moment, to think of a single reason she should fight him.

"We will work it out, you and I," he said. Quiet command
rang in his voice, through her. "It was foretold when we were
children. Never doubt it now."

"Of course," she said, aware of his fingers like hot brands
against her skin—aware, too, of the rich, wild heat that
washed through her because of it. Of how much she had always wanted him, even when she'd believed him to be no
more than a dream. "Because you say so. Does the world always align itself with your wishes, according to your com-
mands?"

"Of course," he said, echoing her, that smile of his lighting up his eyes, broadcasting that calm confidence, that deceptively graceful strength of his. "I am the King."

The shockingly luxurious private jet hovered somewhere high
in the night sky above the Atlantic Ocean, the world shrouded
in black on all sides, but Lara could not sleep as she knew
she should. She stared blindly out the window as the plane
cut through the dark clouds, shivering slightly as reality sank
into her like a great weight.

What had she done? How could she possibly have agreed
to this?

She had spent her whole life avoiding exactly this—her

return to Alakkul. Marlena had spoken of it as if it was the worst possible scenario, the ultimate pit of doom and despair. As if they would die should it happen—or, worse, wish to die. *"Azat will hunt us down and drag us back there,"* she had told the young Lara again and again. *"He will make you one more of his little puppets, who live only to serve him!"*

They had taken Marlena's mother's maiden name as their surname. No more Princess Lara. No more *Your Highness.* Marlena had moved them whenever she felt threatened, whenever she had reason to think the King's goons were drawing near. Always, King Azat was the boogeyman, the monster they sought to avoid. Lara wasn't sure when the crushing fear had started to recede—or why Marlena had finally permitted them to settle down in Denver. She only knew that once she'd finished college, Marlena had seemed far less worried than she'd been before, and far happier to make herself a home in nearby Aspen.

Lara wasn't sure when she'd first started to wonder if, perhaps, Marlena had simply been overreacting. Perhaps there had never been any goons—any escape. Perhaps Marlena had simply wanted a divorce. But thinking such things had always felt deeply disloyal to the only parent she had access to, and felt doubly so now. Lara pushed the thoughts away.

Adel sat not far away, frowning down at the documents before him, a soft reading light surrounding him in a warm halo. Lara could not help but watch him. He was so much more than the cascade of her teenage memories, her teenage feelings, and the simple fact of his commanding presence. He was everything she had been taught to fear about Alakkul—and Alakkulian men in particular. Autocratic bullies, Marlena had said—content to use their power to crush, maim, destroy.

Wasn't that what he'd done today? Wasn't that what she'd let him do? Emotion rose like bile in her throat, and she had to struggle to keep from crying out. She squeezed her eyes shut and tried to breathe.

She did not know this man. She had only the memories she'd held on to for years, and her own sense that she owed Marlena this—that she could not let her mother pay such a high price for their escape. That was all. And yet she had agreed to marry him? To be the queen of a country she hardly remembered—had gone out of her way, in fact, to forget? Lara shifted in her seat and wondered if she would wake up and find herself in her bed at home in Denver—if this was one more of those dreams she'd used to have, all desperate and yearning and dark until she woke, gasping for breath, her heart pounding in her chest.

But when she looked up, she was still on the plane. It was all too real. And Adel was watching her from his place across the cabin, as if he'd heard her very thoughts.

"You should rest," he said. His gray eyes were shadowed now, storm-colored and stern, not silver at all. She did not know why she should feel that as a loss—why she should want to change them back. "You will need your strength, I think, for what lies ahead."

"Thank you," she said past the dryness in her throat and the clutch of panic that still gripped her. "That is very comforting."

"Your father lies in state in the palace," Adel said, his voice giving her no quarter, his hard eyes allowing her no mercy. "He must be buried as his legacy and consequence demand. As his country demands."

Lara opened her mouth to make a wry comment on that—to mention, perhaps, what sort of legacy he'd always held in her mind—but swiftly thought better of it. Adel Qaderi, hand-picked by King Azat to succeed him, always the son to her father that she could never be, was unlikely to find Marlena Canon's stories of the cruelties visited upon her particularly persuasive. Given the way he'd referred to her mother already, however offhandedly, Lara suspected Adel believed a deeply skewed version of reality. He was King Azat's chosen heir!

She knew exactly what he believed: the story her father had told him.

But what if Marlena had made all of that up? a small voice asked. She swallowed. It didn't matter any longer. It couldn't. It was twelve years too late. She would have to go on believing what she'd always believed.

Something must have showed on her face, because his attention seemed to focus in on her then. Too intent. Too demanding. He exuded far too much raw power, even sitting there with his work in front of him, like some kind of common businessman.

Common, Lara thought, with a shaking deep within that she could not quite convince herself was panic, was something Adel Qaderi could never be.

"If you have negative things to say about King Azat, as I can see you do, I suggest you say them to me here," Adel said. His voice was harsh, his gaze frankly condemning. "You are unlikely to find a receptive ear in Alakkul, where he has long been considered a hero as well as a monarch."

"Perhaps," Lara said, conscious of the edge in her voice, her skin prickling with the urge to slap back at that disapproving note in his voice, to defend herself and her mother, "he was a better king than he was a father or a husband." She raised her brows in challenge. "For your country's sake, I certainly hope so."

"And you feel qualified to judge him as a man, as a father?" Lara did not mistake that silky tone for something soft—she could see the steel in his gaze. "You, who showed your daughterly devotion by pretending he did not exist for twelve long years? You, who were not even aware that he was ill, nor that he had died?"

"I do not need to justify myself or the intricacies of my family's dynamics to you," she snapped at him, surprised that his words pricked at her.

His eyes bored into her from across the cabin. Why should

she want to squirm? Why should she feel something far too much like shame? "I witnessed, firsthand, what your abandonment wrought."

"I can imagine how it must have pained him to lose two of his many interchangeable, nameless possessions," Lara said sarcastically.

"Azat will raise you to be nothing more than a pet," Marlena had told her. Repeatedly. *"Meek. Easy. Forever owned and operated at his command, at his disposal. Is that what you want? Is that any kind of life?"*

"Believe me, he knew your name," Adel replied in that low, furious tone. His mouth twisted, and his gaze chilled. "And your mother's."

"My mother is the only hero I'm aware of being related to," Lara threw at him, feeling a desperate, consuming need to defend Marlena. To avenge her. To fight for her, even now, even when she wasn't sure she believed her story. "But that's not something a man like you can understand, can you? The plight of a single mother on her own, forced to run from all she knew—"

"Forced?" Adel laughed, but it was a mirthless sound. "You must be joking. The only thing your mother was ever forced to do was face her own failings as a wife. But she could not handle that, and so she ran from the palace with you rather than deal with the consequences of her behavior." His gaze hardened. "And when I say 'consequences,' let me be clear. I am speaking of her admitted infidelity."

"Don't you dare speak of her!" Lara cried, rising from her chair without knowing she meant to move. Her hands moved of their own accord, out in front of her as if she meant to strike him. As if she dared. And oh, how she wished she dared! "You know nothing about her, or me! You have no idea what our life was like!"

"No," he said with a seething sort of impatience, and that hard gaze that seemed to arrow into her very core, "I know what your life *should* have been. I know what was stolen from you. And from the King. And from your people." He made an abortive gesture with one hand. "I know that when the country needed you, you—*the Crown Princess of Alakkul*—were toiling away in some pedestrian job, in some life far beneath your station, acting as if you were nothing more than a run-of-the-mill, anonymous nobody. Instead of who you really are. The last Alakkulian princess. The dawning of a new age for our people. How can you possibly defend the woman who so dishonored you?"

There was a searing kind of silence. As if the whole world hung there between them, changing even as she tried to breathe. Lara could feel her pulse hit hard against her neck, her ribs, her wrists. And between her legs. Just like his voice.

"My mother *saved* me!" She could not take his words in, could not let them register. She could only remember the stories, so many stories, and the nights her mother had wailed and screamed and cursed, and there had only been Lara to comfort her. Had it all been lies? *All of it?*

"From what, exactly?" Adel demanded, incredulous, sitting forward in his chair. "Your wealth? Your heritage? Everything that should have been yours? *Me?* Are you certain she is the hero of this story—and not its villain?"

"I know all about the life I might have led, had I languished in that horrible place," Lara threw at him. She wanted to hurt him back. To make him pay for saying these things to her, and she did not want to think about why she blamed him. "I thank God every day that my mother saved me from that. From you—a fate worse than death!"

"Says someone who has never faced death," Adel said smoothly, his voice a dark current that moved over her, through her. That made her feel things she hated—that made her hate herself. Things that made no sense. "Because had you done so, you would not make such naive statements. Did your mother fill your head with this foolishness? That *death* was preferable to your birthright? To a marriage that at sixteen you wanted desperately?"

"A birthright—a marriage—that would have been nothing but a prison term," Lara retorted, desperate to strike back at him, to make him as off-balance as she felt, somehow, as some kind of retaliation. Because she could remember, now, that desperate, dazzled yearning for him. Oh, how she had wanted him! It made her even angrier now. "A whole life shut away in a gilded cage—never allowed to think or dream or *live*. Trained from a girl to be nothing more than a biddable wife, a possession, a *thing*. The pawn or the prize for men like you. No, thank you."

"You say things you cannot possibly mean," Adel said, his voice growing softer, more dangerous. She was reminded, suddenly, that he was a warrior first, a king second. That he had all manner of weapons at his disposal. His head tilted slightly as he regarded her. "When I kissed you, you cried tears of joy. When I took your hands in mine, you trembled. You were sixteen and in love with me, and I remember the truth of what was between us even if you do not. She took that from you, too. And from me."

"No," Lara said, her hands in fists at her sides, afraid to let his words penetrate—to let herself remember the things he did. "I was a teenager. I was in love with the idea of love. You were incidental. My mother did us both a favor!"

"There are any number of words I could use to describe your mother, Princess," Adel said in a deadly tone. The hairs on Lara's neck stood at attention. "But I will refrain from using them in your presence because they are disrespectful." His eyes flashed. "Not to her, about whom I could not care less. But to you, my future queen."

"Your mean your possession," Lara flashed at him. Her temper was a live thing, fusing with her panic, her fear, the memories of her sixteen-year-old heart. Making her too reckless, too thoughtless. But she couldn't stop—as if she was as desperate now as she had been then. "Your pawn. Your *object*."

"If that is how you see yourself, who am I to contradict you?" he asked, but she could see the temper he kept at bay. It was in the fire in his cold eyes, the set of his hard jaw. "Demean yourself as you see fit."

"You would love that, I'm sure," she seethed at him, drifting closer to his seat, so focused on her anger that she hardly noticed what she was doing. *Or maybe you just want to be close to him, as you always have,* a small voice whispered, daring her even closer. "Why don't I just bow down and give you all the power? Why don't you just treat me like one more mindless marionette who dances on a string for your pleasure?"

She did not like the way he stared at her, the way his hard mouth curved into an even harder smile, the way his gray eyes glittered. She did not understand the loud beating of her heart, much less the way she shook.

She did not *want* to understand.

"Ah, Princess," he said, his voice a low growl that seemed to reverberate through her like a drum. "You should not tease."

And then, with an economy of movement and a shattering male grace, he hauled her into his arms, across his lap, and took her mouth with his.

CHAPTER FOUR

LARA had no time to react.

His mouth was on hers, hard and demanding. One hand held her at the nape of her neck, the other at her hip, holding her fast against the granite expanse of his chest.

His kiss was possessive, angry, hot. Nothing like the sweet kisses they'd stolen so long ago—and yet so much more. Lara could do nothing but glory in it, even as her hands rose to his shoulders—whether to push him away or pull him closer she would never know.

Fire rolled through her, scorching her, making her forget everything except the power of his kiss, the dark mastery of it, the tight, lush angle of his mouth, his heat and his taste and the breathtakingly sensual way he held her.

As if he had all the time in the world to explore her mouth.

As if tasting her was a matter of critical importance.

As if he was already inside her, claiming her, taking her, making her his in every way.

She felt more than branded. More than stamped, somehow, as his.

She felt more than the molten, restless heat between her legs, more than the wild drumming of her heart, more than his hardness beneath her, against her.

He kissed her as if he knew her as well as he claimed he did. As if it had been only moments since the last time he'd kissed her, instead of years. As if they had always been destined to come together like this, mouth to mouth, body to body, passion to passion.

As if they were meant for each other. As if he was, finally, the home she'd spent her whole life searching for.

It was that last, impossible thought that had her rearing back, her head caught fast in his large hand, to look into his silver eyes.

She hardly knew herself, much less him. Their history was lost in the mists of time, a teenage fantasy at best. This was all too real. Too much.

"You can't..." she began, but she had no idea what to say. How could she tell him that kissing him made the world fall away? That she forgot who she was? That she wanted nothing more than to burrow into him, lose herself in him, and the very madness of that idea made her tremble with need?

Just like before.

"Kiss me," he urged her, as if he knew all the things she could not say.

It was not until he closed the gap between them again, that fascinating mouth so hot against her own, so right, that she realized he had stopped speaking English yet again. And more to the point—so had she.

She tasted sweet, just like he remembered. Like ripe summer berries and the kick of *woman* beneath it. She went to his head like wine.

Adel wanted her, this untutored, disrespectful princess of his, more than he could remember wanting another. More than he wanted almost anything else. Her lush little body curled into his, against his, as if she too could not get close enough. As if she felt the same rush of desire that surged through him, making him want to forget himself in her.

Just as it should be. Just as it had been.

He let his hands travel over the body he'd longed to possess totally for so many years. He tested the shape of her full breasts, traced the indentation of her waist, learned the intoxicating swell of her hips. She writhed against him, her lushness against his hardness, driving him ever closer to distraction. And still he kissed her, again and again, drinking from her, reveling in her, making her pant and shake against him.

Again, he felt triumph beat like a drum in him. She was his. She was *his*, and she was more than simply this lush body, this elemental passion. She was the dream of his family for generations. She was the throne of Alakkul. She was his destiny taking shape, finally, after so many years spent preparing for it.

She was the only woman he had ever loved. His queen. *His*.

Which meant he could wait a little bit longer before taking her, though he longed to do it now with every inch of his body, the want of her so fierce, so total, there was a long moment he was not at all certain he could let go of her.

She would be his queen.

She made a soft sound of distress when he tore his mouth from hers, and set her away from him. Her silver-blue eyes were wide and dark, her mouth damp and slightly swollen from his kisses. He felt a sharp surge of possessiveness, of desire. He let his hands rest on her shoulders for a moment, then dragged his thumb over her full lower lip, smiling when she shuddered her response.

"Not here," he said, though it was more difficult than it should have been. "Not now."

She blinked, and he could see when she understood him. Color flooded her face, staining her cheeks as she disentangled herself from him.

"You are getting ahead of yourself," she snapped at him, in what he imagined she intended to be quelling tones, and might have been, were she not still breathless.

His smile deepened, and he let his hand drop to her breasts, where her nipples stood out, proud and taut, against the tissue-thin fabric of her shirt. He traced one hard peak with the pad of his finger.

"Am I?" he asked lazily.

"You are a pig!" she hissed, rearing back from him, putting space between them and climbing to her feet.

Adel let her go. Temper made her coloring that much more dramatic, and in any case, he had tasted the sweet honey of her desire. He could see the way she trembled, the way her eyes kept returning to his mouth. He knew the truth. If she had to hate him, if she had to pretend—well, he knew what her body wanted, what it needed. It would betray her easily enough.

"Calm yourself," he suggested mildly.

She looked murderous for a moment. He heard her sharp intake of breath, and then, stiffly, she gathered herself, her flowing dark curls like a curtain around her slender shoulders. He watched her spine straighten. She stood near the line of windows, and looked away from him for a moment. Then another. Biting her tongue, he had no doubt.

"I will not rut with my future queen here," he told her when she turned toward him again, her gaze shuttered, as if she could hide from him. "On a plane, God knows where. You deserve greater respect from me than that."

"How interesting," she said, her voice sharp. "*Respect* seems an awful lot like *control.*"

"I am sorry to disabuse you of your deep-held fantasies," he said softly, "but the truth is that I do not wish for you to be my puppet, dancing on a string or otherwise. I want you to be my wife. My queen." He smiled slightly. "The dancing is purely optional."

"And what about what I want?" Her voice was strained. Stark. He did not think this was defiance—he thought this was something else, perhaps even the thing that haunted her, making her eyes too big in her face, her skin too pale. Would she tell him what it was? Would she learn to trust him?

He wanted her to do so more than he wanted to admit.

"Tell me what you want," he said, his voice hushed, as he struggled with urges inside of him he could not entirely understand. "If I can give it to you, I will."

"Perhaps I wish to rut with you, right here and right now," she said, her eyes meeting his boldly. He could not help but harden even further at that—almost to the point of pain—as he imagined her astride him, beneath him, her lush mouth fastened to his, her softness spread out before him. "Why do you get to make the decisions? Am I to be your queen or your slave?"

He could think of several answers to that question, but chose to take the query seriously.

"We will rule together," he said. "As tradition requires."

"What does 'together' mean to an Alakkulian male, I wonder?" she mused, her eyes narrowed. "I somehow doubt it means the same thing to you as it does to me. What if we wish to rule differently? What if you are wrong? Who gets to decide?"

Their eyes met, held. The attraction that sizzled between them seemed to intensify, seemed to beat at him with hot, dangerous flames. Why did her anger, her restless intelligence, make him want her all the more?

"I suspect," he said after a moment, "that you already know the answer."

She made a scoffing noise, and folded her arms over her chest. "What a surprise," she said after a moment, in a bitter sort of tone.

And something in him tore free. He could not have said why. It was her defiance, perhaps, or—more curious—his surprising, continuing sympathy for her plight. He felt more for her than he had ever felt for another, even across these long years of separation. He wanted her as he had never wanted any other woman. And still she looked at him as if he was the enemy. As if she did not quite grasp who he was.

Perhaps it was time to tell her. To remind her.

He was on his feet before he knew he meant to move—a shocking deviation from the usual iron control he maintained over himself and anyone in his orbit. He stalked over to her, enjoying the way her expression changed, became far more wary, though she only squared her shoulders as he came closer. She did not cower. She did not run. She only waited, and he knew she was more his queen in that moment than she realized.

He moved closer, deliberately stepping into her space, so she was trapped against the wall of the plane and forced to look up at him. He placed a hand on the smooth surface of the bulkhead on either side of her head, framing her face, and leaned in.

"If you kiss me again," she told him fiercely, "I will bite you."

"You will not." But his attention moved to her mouth. "Unless I ask you to."

"Stop trying to intimidate me," she ordered him, but once again there was that tell-tale breathiness in the voice she'd clearly meant to sound stern. He smiled, and allowed himself to touch her hair—pulling one dark black curl between his fingers, running the thick silk over his lips, and inhaling the scent. Mint and honey. *His princess.*

"Stop it!" she whispered, her eyes wide. Wary.

Wanting, he thought, with no little satisfaction.

"Listen to me," he said. He let the curl drop from his hand, but he did not move back. Her hands moved, as if she went to push him away but thought better of touching him. "I am not one of your American men. I am not politically correct."

"Really?" Her tone was dry. Defiant. "I hadn't noticed."

He liked being so close to her. More, perhaps, than he should. He could smell her, almost taste her, feel the heat of her. But because indulging himself would lead precisely where he did not wish to go, not yet, he leaned away, still keeping his arms on either side of her, but removing his mouth from the temptation of hers.

"I am not modern." His voice was low. As if he offered her his confession, though the very thought was absurd. "I cannot pretend to be to save your feelings, or to coddle your Western sensibilities."

"Is that what's been happening so far?" she asked, her brows arching. She shook her head. "The mind balks. What's next? The barbarian horde?"

"I was trained to be a soldier since I was a child," he told her, not certain why he'd started there. Not at all easy with the baffling urge to share himself with her, to let her see him, know him, as he'd thought she might long ago. Not sure he wanted to examine that urge more closely. "A barbarian by your measure, I suppose. My parents sent me to the palace when I was still a child, barely five years old. I was raised to be a weapon. A machine. One of the King's personal guard."

She only stared at him. "The *cadre*," she murmured. And he knew that she remembered the tight band of warriors who had shadowed her father's every movement, each one of them more dangerous than the next, whose honor and duty it was to accompany the King wherever he went. To lay down their lives for him at a moment's notice. To live in service to his whims. He had been the youngest ever inducted into the *cadre*'s elite ranks. Perhaps she remembered that, too.

"I was taught to sever all emotional ties," he continued, fighting the urge to touch her soft skin, to feel her heartbeat with his hands. "I learned to focus only on one goal—protecting and serving my king, my country. I did so, gladly. I wanted no greater glory than that. Until your father gave me you."

"I was not his to give," she said, but her voice was soft,

as if she felt this same, strange tenderness. Her eyes moved over his face.

"And you wanted me, too," he reminded her. "Duty and desire, all at once. We were lucky, Princess."

Memory and desire shimmered between them, like need. Like heat.

"I remember you, Adel," she admitted in a stark whisper. She swallowed, nerves and memories and something dark in her gaze. "I do. But that doesn't mean I can be who you want me to be. Maybe not ever."

"I will protect my country," he said, though he suspected that was not an answer she would like—that she might not even understand why he said it. Or the stark truth of it. "No matter the cost. Nothing means more to me than that."

"Not even the throne?" she asked, incisive yet again.

"There is nothing I would not do for Alakkul, nothing I would not sacrifice, and no one I would not betray in service to my country, if my duty to my country demanded it." His voice was so sure, coming from deep within him. Why did he want her to understand? Why did he want her this much—so all-consumingly? So overwhelmingly? She gazed up at him and there was an expression on her face that made something in him twist over on itself. "I cannot pause in this and make you easy with the role you must assume. I would not even know where to begin."

Something pulled taut between them, dark and glittering. She pulled in a breath, then another, her gaze unreadable.

"Don't worry," she said, her voice tense. Almost sad. "I told you—I remember. I know exactly who you are."

"No," he said, his voice harder than it should have been, though she did not flinch—and he admired her for it, almost grudgingly. "You don't. But you will, soon enough."

Lara woke slowly, aware that she was stiff and that her dreams had been wild pageants, complicated and emotional and much too heavy. It took long moments to dispel them, to remember where she was, and why.

And then she looked out the window and wondered if she'd woken up at all.

The great valley of Alakkul, mystical and secretive, spread out before her—ringed by the sharp, snow-capped mountains on all sides. Her half-remembered homeland sparkled in the morning light, white snow and deep green fields, the rich browns and greens of the forests, and the deep crystal blues of the clear mountain lakes. From high above, she could see the remotest villages and the farmer's fields, the bustling towns and the bigger, busier cities, tucked into the foothills and spreading across the valley floor.

She did not merely *see*, Lara thought in a mix of elation and despair—she *felt*. It was as if a great wall within her, one she hadn't known was there, began to crack into pieces, to fall. Her eyes drank in the bright red flowers that spread across the high mountain fields like a boisterous carpet in the summer sun, so cheerful against the deep greens of the grassy meadows and the smoky blues of the far mountains. All of it seemed to resonate within her, as if she had been hiding all her life and only in this moment had stepped into the light.

You are being fanciful, she cautioned herself, but the plane was dropping closer and closer to the earth, and she could not tell the difference between memory and reality—she could only feel. Too much. Much too much. The spires and steeples of the sacred city appeared before her, until they flew directly over the ancient palace itself, its turrets and towers arching gracefully toward the summer sky above.

Home, she thought, and felt that word ricochet through her, leaving marks.

Lara found she was holding her breath, but even that could not seem to stop the great swell of emotion inside of her, that seemed to rip her into pieces. She could not tear her eyes away, not even when the plane continued its inexorable descent and bumped gently down on the runway.

She could not breathe. She was afraid she might be sobbing and she couldn't even tell for sure, because her ears were ringing and she could not *think*—and the plane was taxiing to a stop and this was really happening. She was really, truly here, after twelve long years.

She rose in a daze, and followed the smiling air hostess out into the morning light. It was so blinding. So clear and pure. The high mountain air was so crisp. She walked down the stairs to the tarmac, and noticed almost distantly the way the people standing there reacted, bowing and crying out her name in their language. But her brain couldn't quite process what they said. What that meant. Her attention was on the view all around her—the mountains, the trees, the magical palace—all of it clearly Alakkul and nowhere else. She knew, suddenly, that she would know where she was if she was blind. She could smell it, sense it. Taste it. Feel it deep in her bones.

Home, that voice whispered inside of her again, ringing through her. It shook her to the core. Changed her, she thought irrationally. Changed her forever.

It was only then that she heard someone else come down the metal stairs behind her. She turned, and there was Adel, broad and dark against the summer morning. His attention was entirely focused on her, and she felt herself burst into a riot of flames as he drew closer. How could he do that, she wondered helplessly, even now, when she felt both more lost—and more found—than she ever had before?

He stopped before her, and reached over to take her hand. She should stop him, she thought. She had not yet processed any of the things that had happened, what had passed between them, and yet she did not pull her hand away. She couldn't seem to do it. She couldn't seem to *want* to do it. How could she feel safe with this man, when she knew all too well that was the one thing she was not? Once again, she was aware of the people standing at a respectful distance, all of them bowing again, some even sinking into deep curtseys. But Adel was beside her, his hand around hers, and she felt the panic inside of her ease. Just as it always had, even twelve years ago. As if he could make the world stop at his command. She remembered the feeling. She felt it now.

Adel raised her hand to his lips and then, impossibly, his dark eyes meeting hers for a searing moment, bowed his head over it.

"The King is dead," he said in ringing tones that carried across the tarmac, perhaps rebounding off the looming mountain guardians of her childhood to lodge in her soul.

His dark eyes connected with hers, silver and serious, and made her stomach twist inside of her.

"Long live the Queen!" he cried in the same voice, and turned, presenting her to the assembled throng. There were flashbulbs. Applause. More bowing, and some cheers.

"Adel..." But she didn't know what she meant to say.

"Welcome home, Princess," he murmured, his hand warm around hers, his eyes dark gray, his mouth that familiar unyielding line.

It made the hard knot of panic inside of her ease. She felt herself breathe in, felt her shoulders settle, as if he'd directed her to do so. As if he made it possible. Just as he'd done long ago, this not-quite-stranger. He bowed his head again, and that firm mouth curved slightly.

"My queen," he said.

And, somehow, made all of it both real, and all right.

CHAPTER FIVE

THE funeral was an ornate affair, with priests and dignitaries and far too many eyes turned in the direction of the new Queen of Alakkul.

Lara sat in the great cathedral in the position of honor, with Adel close to her side, both of them outfitted in the finest Alakkulian garments. The fabric of her severe black gown felt rich and sumptuous against her skin, despite the fact the occasion was so grim. But she could not let herself think about that, not even as the assembled masses rose to sing an ancient hymn of loss and mourning and faith in the afterlife. She could only bow her head and try to calm herself. Try to breathe—try to stay upright. Beside her, Adel shifted, and briefly squeezed her hand with his.

She dared not look at him directly, no matter how his touch moved her—how it seemed to trickle through her veins, warming and soothing her. A quick glance confirmed he looked too uncompromisingly handsome, too disturbing in his resplendent military regalia, as befitted the highest ranking member of the country, save, she supposed with the still-dazed part of her brain that was capable of thinking of these things, herself. She was afraid that she would stare at him too long and disgrace herself.

As, of course, no small part of her wanted to do. Anything to avoid the reality of her father's death. Of the fact that this was his funeral, and she had hardly known him. Would, now, never know him. She had hated the man passionately for almost as long as she could remember, she had gone out of her way to do so to better please and placate her mother, so why did she feel this strange hollowness now? Did she believe the things that Adel had said about Marlena? If not, then surely she should feel either some small measure of satisfaction or nothing at all?

The truth was, she did not have the slightest idea what she felt, much less what she *should* feel. How could she? She had been in this strange place, with its surprisingly fierce kicks of nostalgia and odd flashes of memories, for under forty-eight hours. She had been whisked from the airfield to the palace, her meager possessions placed carefully in a sumptuous suite she only vaguely recalled had once been her mother's—and soon augmented by the kinds of couture ensembles more appropriate to her brand-new, unwanted position. She had been waited upon by fleets of bowing, eager attendants, who were there to see to needs she was not even aware she ought to have. Her wardrobe. Her appointments. Her new, apparently deeply complicated life.

Her first official duty as the new Queen was this funeral. This sending off of a man who clearly inspired loyalty—devotion—from his people, and from the man who stood beside her now. Lara did not know how to reconcile the man they spoke of here, in hushed and reverent tones, with the monster her mother had conjured for her for so many years. She did not know how to feel about the disparity. She did not want to believe Adel's story of her mother's infidelity—but could not seem to put it out of her head.

She did not know how to feel about anything.

Her orderly, comfortable life in Denver was gone as if it had never existed. The only constant was the man at her side, and the only thing she knew she felt about him was a deep and abiding confusion. Her body still longed for him, in deep, consuming ways that startled her. Her mind rebelled against everything he stood for and his own designs upon her. And yet her heart seemed to hurt inside her chest when she pictured him as a child, forced to play war games in the royal palace, torn from his own family when he'd been hardly more than a toddler. It seemed to beat faster when she remembered their first kiss, her very first kiss ever, so sweet and forbidden, in a hidden corner of the castle ballroom when she had been just sixteen.

She did not have to examine these things more closely to know that she was undeniably, and disastrously, consumed with the man who had an intolerable level of control over this new life of hers.

The question, she asked herself as the service ended and the procession began, and he was still the only thing that she could seem to focus on, was what, if anything, did she plan to do about it?

Much later, after King Azat had been interred in his final resting place beneath the stones of the ancient mausoleum and all the polite words had been spoken to all the correct people, Lara found herself still in her new, stiff black gown, standing awkwardly in one of the palace's smaller private salons.

Across from her, framed by the gilt and gold that graced every spare inch of the walls and floors and ceilings of this fairy-tale place, looking every inch the new King, Adel poured himself a drink. He did so with his customary masculine grace, and Lara could not understand why even something so simple, so mundane, as this man splashing amber-colored liquor into a crystal tumbler should cause her blood to heat. He turned to look at her as if he'd felt the weight of her gaze, his expression that same watchful, careful calmness that she knew all too well by now.

Knew, but could not quite read. Why should that make her heart speed up in her chest?

Lara felt as awkward and as stiff as the fussy room they stood in, as the elegant gown she still wore when she longed for something more casual, more comfortable. Her hands moved restlessly before her, plucking at the fabric of her long skirt. She could not seem to keep still. She wandered the edges of the small salon, stopping before the great windows that looked out over the ancient city, all the spires and rooftops gleaming white and blue as the sun dipped toward the western mountains. It looked indescribably foreign to her eyes, and yet some part of her thrilled to the sight, as if she was as much a part of the landscape as he was. As if it was in her blood.

"They cheered," she said, not knowing she meant to speak, not knowing her voice would sound so insubstantial. She swallowed, and reached a hand toward the window, the glass cool beneath her reaching fingers. "When we were in the car, heading back here. Why would they do that?"

"You are their princess, now their queen," Adel said, his even voice filling the small room, pressing against her ears, and burrowing beneath her skin. "The last of an ancient and revered bloodline, the daughter of a beloved ruler now lost to them. You were stolen away from them when you were just a girl. They celebrate your safe return to the place you belong." He paused for a moment. "Your home."

She looked over her shoulder at him, not knowing why she trembled, why his eyes seemed so sure, and yet managed to make her feel so raw inside. She wanted to speak—perhaps she wanted to scream—but nothing moved past her lips.

"They adore you," he said.

"Not me." She shook her head, swallowed. "Some idea of what I should be, perhaps, but not me."

He heard the dark, wild panic in her voice, and moved toward her, though he had promised himself he would not touch her again. A promise he had already broken repeatedly. In the cathedral. In the car. In the endless reception. He, who held his vows to be sacred. And still, he moved behind her, setting his untouched drink on a side table and letting his hands come to rest on her shoulders.

"It becomes easier," he murmured, close to the perfect shell of her ear, the tempting, elegant line of her neck.

"How do you stand it?" she asked, her eyes fixed on the city outside the windows, as if one of the most beautiful views in the kingdom disturbed her. "All that…expectation?"

She sounded torn. Terrified. And he wanted to soothe her. He wanted to kiss the panic from her body, make her forget herself and the demands of her station. But he could not afford that kind of misstep. Not now, when the King was buried and gone. When so much remained at stake.

"We will marry at the end of the week," he said gruffly. "There is no time to waste."

He felt the shock move through her body, like an electrical current.

"What is the hurry?" she asked, turning so she faced him, not seeming to notice that his hands remained on her, sliding down to hold her upper arms in his palms. "Surely what matters is that I am here. Must we force all of these changes into only a handful of days?"

Her voice caught slightly on the word *changes.* He hated himself for pushing her, but he had no choice. He had been bound over to his country so long ago now he no longer remembered any other way. There were far greater things than the hurt feelings of one woman to worry about, even if it was this one, and far more important things to consider than his abiding desire to comfort her. There was much more at stake than these quiet moments that he knew, somehow, he would never get back.

But he had never had any choice.

"The ceremony will be in the cathedral, as tradition demands," he said as if he had not heard her. She frowned up at him. He found himself frowning back at her, a surge of sudden, unreasonable anger moving through him, though he knew it was not her he was angry with. "Will you fight this, too, Princess? Will we see who wins this latest battle? I should let you know that I am unlikely to be as easy on you as I have been. My patience for these games of yours wears thin."

For a moment she looked as if he'd slapped her. Her face whitened, then blazed into color. She pressed her lips together for a moment, and then her silvery eyes seemed to look straight into him. Through him.

"What is this?" she asked, in a calm voice that sounded eerily like his own. As if she'd learned it from him. "What are you not telling me?"

He did not know, in that moment, whether he wanted to strangle her or tumble her to the floor. He was appalled at the riot of emotion inside of him. He stepped back, forcing himself to let go of her. Making himself breathe and regain his own control.

He had always known he would marry this woman, that she was his. And he would make that happen, one way or another. The fact that he loved her, that he burned for her—that was incidental. It had to be.

"Many things," he answered finally. "Did you imagine it would be otherwise? Have you shared all your secrets with me?"

Her wide eyes searched his, then dropped. He saw her pull in a steadying breath, and wanted to touch her—but did not.

"It occurs to me that I am already the Queen," she said after a long moment, looking every inch of her heritage, her head held proudly, her inky black hair in that elegant twist. "While, if I am not mistaken, you must marry me to become king."

"You are correct," he said silkily, watching her closely, the warrior instinct stirring to life within his blood. Was that pride he felt? That she was a worthy opponent even today of all days? "Your ancestors have held the throne of Alakkul since the tenth century."

Her head tilted slightly to one side as she considered him. "And what is to prevent me choosing a different king?" she asked in that soft voice that he did not mistake for anything but a weapon. "One I prefer to you?"

He felt himself smile, not nicely. Far stronger men had quailed before that smile, but Lara only watched him, her eyes blazing with a passion he did not entirely understand. But oh, how he longed to bathe in it.

Soon, he told himself. *Soon enough.*

"Theoretically," he said, "you can choose any king you wish."

She blinked, and then seized on the important part of what he'd just said. "But not in practice?" she asked.

"There is the matter of your vows and our betrothal," he said. "Honor matters more here, to those people who loved you enough to cheer you in the streets, than in your other world. Breaking your word and defying your late father's wishes would cause a deep and lasting scandal." He shrugged. "But you are American now, are you not? Perhaps you will not mind a scandal."

"I think I'll announce to the world at large that the new Queen of Alakkul is in need of a king," she said, her eyes bright, daring him. "Surely any number of suitors will present themselves. It can be like my own, personal reality show."

She expected him to react badly, he could tell. But he saw the way her pulse pounded in the tender crook of her neck, and smiled.

"By all means, Princess," he said. "Invite whoever you like to court you."

"You don't mind?" Her voice was ripe with disbelief. "You don't think you're the better choice?"

He laughed, enjoying the way the sound made her frown.

"There is no doubt at all that I am the better choice," he said. "But more than that, I am the only choice."

"According to you," she said, defiant and beautiful.

"No," he said softly. He reached across and traced a simple line along the elegant length of her neck, smiling in satisfaction when she hissed in a breath and goose bumps rose. "According to you," he said, his own body reacting to her arousal. "You have loved me since you were but a girl. You will again. Your body is already there." He did not smile now—he met her gaze with his own, steady and sure. "You will not pick another king."

That bald statement seemed to hang between them, making the air hard to breathe. Lara's stomach hurt, and her hands balled into fists.

"Why must I marry anyone?" she asked, her voice low and intent, growing hoarse with the emotion she fought to conceal, even as her body rioted, proving his words to be true no matter how she longed to deny them. "Why can't I simply be queen on my own?"

But Adel only shook his head, in that infuriating manner of his that made her itch to explode into some kind of decisive action. But then again, perhaps touching him was not a good idea.

"Why should I trust anything you say?" she threw at him, angry beyond reason, dizzy with all she wanted and would not allow herself. "You've done nothing but lie to me from the start!"

"I will do whatever it takes to secure the throne and protect this country," he threw back at her. Did she imagine the hint of darker emotion in his voice? Flashing in his gray eyes? Or did she only *want* it to be there?

"You are exactly like him," she said, her voice a low, intense throb of all the pain she had not been able to admit she felt today. All the loss and the bewilderment, and her inability to understand why she should even care that King Azat was dead. Why should it matter to her? Why should she be questioning her mother's motives? And why should she feel so betrayed that Adel was the same kind of man, when he had never pretended to be anything else? When he had as good as told her that he would do just what he had done? When he—like her father before him—cared only and entirely about the damned throne to this godforsaken place?

Hadn't her mother told her this would happen, years before? *"He picked another snake for you, Lara—just like himself!"* she'd hissed.

"If you mean your father," Adel said evenly, the suggestion of ice in his voice, "I will accept the compliment."

"He forced me into this years ago, on my sixteenth birthday," she said dully, wondering why her heart felt broken—why it should even be involved. "Didn't you know? That was when my mother knew we had to escape. She refused to let me—"

"Please spare me these fantasies." His voice was a hard whip of dismissal. Startled, she noticed his eyes had turned to flint. "Your mother left because her extramarital dalliances were discovered. She took you with her as insurance, because she knew that if she stayed here she would have been turned away from the palace in shame. Never deceive yourself on this point. She knew that as long as you were with her, your father would never cut off her funds. Just as she knew he was too concerned with a daughter's feelings for her mother to separate you."

"What?" She couldn't make sense of that. She literally could not process his words. "What are you—? We lived on the run for years! We had to hide from his goons!"

"There was never one moment of your life that the palace did not know where you were," Adel said coolly, every word like a blow. "And I assure you, if your father wanted his 'goons' to secure you, I would have done so personally years ago. If it was up to me, I would have reclaimed you before your seventeenth birthday."

She couldn't accept what he was saying. Her mind was

reeling, and she shook her head once, hard. Then again, to get rid of the part of her that seemed to bloom in pleasure, at the notion that he'd wanted her so badly.

"You would say anything…" she began, but she was barely speaking aloud.

He took her shoulders in his hands again, tipping her head back, making her look at him. Face to face, hiding nothing. Baring far too much.

"I will lie, cheat, steal," he said. His tone was deceptively soft—with that uncompromising edge beneath. "Whatever it takes. But you will marry me."

"I wouldn't be so sure about that!" she hissed, but it was all bravado. Inside she was awash in confusion. Full of the possibility that he, unlike her father and even unlike her mother, had wanted her after all. But unable to let herself really accept that possibility—unable to believe it.

She knew what he meant to do even as his hands tightened on her shoulders, even as his hard mouth dropped toward hers. She knew, and yet she did nothing to evade it.

In truth, she did not want to evade him.

And so he kissed her. That same fire. That same punch and roll. Even now, even here, she burned.

She did not know what that meant. She did not want to think anymore. She did not want to feel. She wanted to lock herself away somewhere—to escape.

But he raised his head, and his eyes were dark gray and too capable of reading too much, his mouth in that grim line that called to her despite everything.

"That proves nothing," she said, because she had to say something—she had to pretend.

"Keep telling yourself that, Princess," he said in that dark, quiet voice that made her alive and bright with need. "If it helps."

CHAPTER SIX

THE day of her wedding dawned wet and cold.

Was it childish that she wanted the weather to be an omen?

A summer storm had swept in from the mountains, shrouding the ancient city in a chilly fog that perfectly suited Lara's mood. She was up before the gray dawn, staring broodingly out her windows, feeling like a princess in one of those old fairy-tales her mother had given her to read when she was a child.

It did not do much to brighten her outlook when she reflected that she was, in fact, a princess locked away in a castle and about to be married off to a suitor not of her choosing. That in her case, those old stories were real.

No matter how little it all *felt* real. No matter how much she still wanted to jolt awake and find herself back in her safe, small life in Denver. The little apartment she'd barely tolerated, and now missed. The job and the friends and the *life* that she had treasured, because it was hers. Because she had not had to run from anything anymore. She had been so proud of that. Of what she'd built when Marlena had let them stop running.

Marlena…who might not be at all who she'd claimed to be for so long. Who Lara had had no choice but to believe.

She tucked her knees up beneath her on her window seat and took in the luxury that dripped from every inch of the suite all around her—the cascade of window treatments in gold and cream, the tapered bed posts, the ornamentation of every surface, every detail. What terrified her was how, every day, the real world seemed further and further away. She spoke less English. She found her new clothes less uncomfortable. She forgot.

How soon would she forget what was truly important? How soon would she forget herself completely?

But then the door swung open, and she was no longer alone. And it was, after all, her wedding day.

She was bathed, slathered in ointments and perfumes, and dressed in a gown so beautiful, so light and airy, that it should have taken her breath away. It made her look like a dream. Like another fairy-tale princess. Her hair was curled, piled onto her head, and bedecked with fine jewels and a tiara that one of her attendants told her, with a smile, had once belonged to Cleopatra herself. There was a part of her that longed to believe such a story, that wanted to revel in the very idea of it. But when she looked at herself in the mirror, she hardly recognized herself.

If she allowed herself to disappear inside this dream, the dream she'd cherished as a girl and hardly believed could be happening now, how would she ever wake up? *Could* she ever wake up? Would she want to?

By the time they had finished with all their ministrations, the bright summer sun had burned away the morning fog, and as Lara was driven outside the palace gates it was as if she drove directly into the happily-ever-after portion of all those old fairy-tales she couldn't seem to put from her mind. The people of Alakkul crowded the streets, cheering and waving. The sun streamed down from the perfect blue sky above. She even thought she heard birds singing sweetly in the trees as she climbed the steps to the great cathedral. Everything was perfect, save for the stone inside her chest where her heart should be, and the fact that she desperately did not want to do this.

Yet…was that true?

She did not break away from her fleet of handlers. She did not pick up her heavy skirts and run. She did not even stop walking, step by measured step, toward her doom. And when she entered the cathedral and saw the figure standing so tall and proud at the altar, she knew why.

He stood at the head of the long aisle, where a few days before her father's coffin had been laid out for all to see. Where, so many years ago, she had stood with him once before, in the very same spot, and dreamed of exactly this moment. Yearned for it. Was it the echo of those long-ago dreams that kept her moving, as if it was the very blood in her veins? Or was it the way he turned and looked at her, an expression she could not read on his hard face as she drew close?

He held out his hand, his gray eyes serious and steady on hers—just as he had done in that parking lot in Denver. It seemed like a different life to her now, a different person altogether. She could not imagine who she'd been, however many days ago, before he'd reappeared in her life and altered it so profoundly. She could not reconstruct that last moment before he'd spoken, when she had been lost in whatever thoughts had consumed her then, when she had forgotten he even existed and had no idea she would ever see him again.

She could not imagine it, and maybe that was what compelled her to reach across the distance between them, and once again take his hand.

In the end, it was quick. Too quick.

The priests intoned the sacred words. Adel stood quietly beside her, yet she was so aware of him. Of his slow, deep breathing. Of his broad shoulders, his impressive height. Of the fierce, compelling strength that was so much a part of him. He was every inch the warrior, even now. Even here.

She could think of him as a warrior. As a king. It was the word *husband* that she could not seem to make sense of—it kept getting tangled up in her head.

And in the final moments, when the priest turned to her

and asked her if she came to this union of her own free will, if she gave herself willingly, Lara looked into Adel's silver eyes, and knew she should say no.

She knew it.

But his gaze was so steady, so calm. So serious.

So very silver, and she felt it wrap around that stone where her heart should be, like a caress. Like a promise.

"He will make you nothing more than a puppet," Marlena had said.

But there were worse things than that, Lara thought. There were worse things than puppetry, and in any case, she could not remember what it had been like before, what it had been like without that calm silver gaze filling her, making her warm from the inside out, making her feel whole when she had not known anything was missing.

She had wanted this man forever.

"Do you come to this moment of your own free will?" the priest asked again.

And she said yes.

"Yes," she said. "I do."

She said yes.

Adel was not aware he had been so tense, so rigid and prepared for battle, until it eased from him. Her voice rang through the cathedral, and sounded deep within him. Unmistakable. Unquestionable.

It was done.

She was his.

He had fulfilled the old King's wishes, to the letter. He had staved off disaster. He had been prepared for anything today. That she might not appear. That she might try to bolt. That she might throw her defiance in his face at this crucial moment. Anything.

He had not been prepared for her beauty. For the way the white gown hugged her figure so tenderly, nor for the way the jewels that adorned her made her seem to sparkle and glow.

He had not, he realized, as he took her hands in his and recited the old words that would make them one, forever, thought much beyond this moment.

He had only thought of marrying her. But he had not spent much time thinking about the marriage itself.

They walked down the aisle, husband and wife, king and queen, and out into their kingdom, together.

She looked up at him, her eyes seeming more blue than silver in the sunlight. Her expression was grave, as if she found this marriage a serious business, requiring much thought and worry.

And he wanted her. God, how he wanted her. Not as the king she had just made him, but as the man who had wanted her since he'd been barely more than a boy. As the man who had tasted her, and touched her, when he had known he should do neither, both twelve years ago and now.

But now...now he did not have to hold back. Now, finally, he could sink into her as he'd longed to do for what felt like much too long. Now he could love her, openly and fully, as he'd always imagined he should.

"Why are you looking at me like that?" she asked, but he could tell she knew.

"Why do you think?" he asked, and smiled. He held her hand in his, and led her toward the waiting motorcade. There was the small matter of the reception to get through, and his coronation. But he was already thinking ahead. He was already imagining how she would taste, how soft her skin would feel beneath his hands. How he would make her cry out his name. How he would make her fall to pieces in his arms.

They stood for a moment, her eyes locked to his, and he felt her tremble slightly in the afternoon sun. As if she could feel it, too. As if she'd finally stopped fighting. As if she was ready, at long last, to be his.

He would make sure of it.

* * *

The High Palace clung to the side of one of the tallest mountains to the west of the capital city. In ancient times, she remembered learning as a child, it had taken many weeks of travel via sure-footed mountain goats and under the protection of guides and priests for the royal family to make it to these heights. It had been a much quicker ride by helicopter.

Standing out on the wide terrace that had been added off the King's suite sometime since her last visit here, Lara looked out across the sweep and grandeur of Alakkul and wondered how she had ever managed to forget it. So many twinkling lights in the dark, mirroring the stars above. The brighter lights of the city, the far-off glimmers of the mountain villages. The crisp, clean air, cool and sweet.

From so high, it looked magical.

Or perhaps she only felt that way, after such a long day immersed in this fairy-tale that was, somehow, her life. It had to be a fairy-tale, because it couldn't possibly be real. None of it felt real. *She* hardly felt real.

Adel moved behind her. She sensed him first—that prickle along her neck, that banked fire blazing to life within her. She let out a breath she had not known she was holding as she felt him step behind her, his warm hands smoothing along the curve of her neck, tracing down over her shoulders.

"Nothing seems real," she heard herself say, so softly she thought for a moment the night breeze stole her words away.

"I assure you, it is." His voice was a low rumble. So amused, and still, her breasts swelled against the bodice of her dress, and that insistent, intoxicating heat pooled lower— became a low ache. He turned her around to face him. "You are my wife."

"And you are now the King of Alakkul," she said, tilting her head back to study that hard, uncompromising face. Did she imagine what looked like tenderness in his eyes, so silver in the light from the candles scattered across the terrace? Or was it that she wanted to see such a thing—needed to believe she could see it?

He reached over and smoothed his hand along her cheek, curving his palm around to cradle her face. There was some part of her that wanted to object. That should *want* to object! She did not have to give in to this heat, this need. He was no brute, no matter how calculating, how ruthless, he might be. Not about something like this. She knew so with a deep, feminine intuition.

If she wanted to stop this, she needed only to open up her mouth and tell him *no*.

But she did not speak. She only gazed at him, all of Alakkul spread out behind her, glimmering in the soft summer night and reflecting in his dark eyes as if it was a part of him. He had smiled at her outside the cathedral, his hard gaze open, and shaken her to her core—because she had seen, in that moment, how happy he was. How happy to look at her, to claim her. It had made her breath catch, her heart swell. It had made her think that he was not, after all, the enemy she wanted to believe he was. That perhaps he never had been.

She stood before him now in a dress that made her feel like the princess she supposed she always had been, technically, but had certainly never felt like before. And he was so devastatingly handsome, so strong and so dangerous, standing before her with that almost-smile on his hard mouth.

As if he knew things that she did not want to know. As if he knew far too much.

Lara gazed at him—and did not say a word.

"Tonight I am only a man," he whispered, his voice a low rasp.

Just as tonight she was finally his woman, as if all the years between them had melted away in his smile. How had she denied him this long?

He pulled her head closer, and bent down to capture her mouth. His kiss was sweet, hot, sending spirals of heat dancing through her body, making her come up on her toes to meet him. She let her hands trail up the tantalizingly hard ridge of his abdomen to his broad chest, reveling in the taut glory of his muscles.

He angled his jaw, and took the kiss deeper. Hotter. Lara felt the world fall away, spinning into nothing, and only belatedly realized he'd swept her into his arms. He kept kissing her as he moved, and she looped her arms around his neck and kissed him back. Again and again, until she found herself on her back in the center of the wide, white bed, with Adel resting snugly between her thighs.

Was she really going to do this? Pretend nothing else mattered but this fire, this need?

"Adel…" she began, but he smiled at her, even as he moved his hips against hers. Lara gasped, and forgot.

She forgot she'd ever wanted to deny him, and instead opened to his every touch. He stripped them both naked with surprising finesse and long, drugging kisses, feasting on every inch of flesh he uncovered. He trailed fire from one breast to the other, then tasted his way down the soft skin of her belly to claim the heat between her legs.

And then he licked his way into the molten core of her, and she forgot her own name.

She shattered around him, caught in a wave of pleasure so intense, so perfect, she was not sure what would be left of her. She was not sure she could survive it.

When she came back to herself, he was poised above her, his hard face sharpened, somehow, with passion.

And she realized it was just beginning.

"You are mine," he said hoarsely, and then he thrust within her.

CHAPTER SEVEN

THE summer wore on as the country settled into its new era, with its new rulers fully ensconced upon the throne, and Adel could not understand why—having finally achieved all he'd ever wanted—the only thing he seemed to think about was his wife.

Not the warring factions that forever threatened to sink the government. Not the leftover yet ever-thorny issues from the various world powers that had tried to take the strategically located Alakkulian Valley in their time. Not the need to protect and support the economy, nor the tendency of some citizens to live as if it were still the tenth century. It was not that he did not care about all of these things. It was just that his focus was Lara. Always Lara.

The way her skin felt against his, naked and soft, hot and delicious. The way her head tipped back in ecstasy, showing the long, elegant line of her neck as she cried out his name. The way her toned, athletic legs wrapped so tightly around his hips. The way she would smile at him, so dreamily, in those stolen moments after they had both reached heaven, her eyes that silver-blue that made his chest expand and ache.

He was enchanted by her, this woman he had loved for so much of his life, and the reality of her far exceeded his fantasies.

It wasn't just the perfection of her body. He even enjoyed her when she argued with him—which was, he reflected as he took in the cross expression she wore as he entered their private breakfast room in the palace—most of the time.

"I don't see the point of being called a queen when all I do is sit around the palace, staring out of windows and boring myself to death," she threw at him with no preamble, her fingers picking at the pastry before her.

"Good morning to you, too," he murmured, settling himself in his usual place opposite her while the servants bustled around him, pouring out his morning coffee and presenting him with a stack of papers for his review.

She ignored him. "I am used to working," she said. "*Doing* something, not sitting around like an ornament attached to your lapel!"

"Then do something," he suggested, picking up his coffee and eyeing her. She made his heart swell with what he could only describe as gladness. Most women cowered before him, or fell all over themselves in an attempt to please him. Never this one. She was bold. Brash. Unafraid. "You are the Queen. You can do as you like."

"Perhaps I wish to rule, as you do," she said, with a sideways glance at him, and he had a sudden image of what it might be like with this woman at his side forever, on the throne and in his bed—this warrior queen he had never expected would grow to be so strong. And yet he loved it. Her.

He shrugged. "You have an affinity for tedious meetings, day after day, with puffed-up, pompous men?" he asked mildly. Not his Lara, he thought. She would shred them with her sharp tongue, and he would laugh in admiration, and whole decades of careful diplomacy would go up in smoke. "Men who will insult you and berate you, who you cannot treat as you would like to do? This calls to you?"

She let out a sigh. "No," she said after a long moment. "Not really."

"Because, Princess, though your charms are many indeed, I do not count among them a particular gift for the diplomatic arts." He smiled when her gaze sharpened on his. "This is not a flaw. You are too honest for politics. One of us should be."

He could feel the tension rise between them then, that tautening of the air, that narrowing of focus until he knew nothing but her face. The swell of her lips. The shine of temper in her gaze. The sweep and fall of her black curls.

He knew her so well now. He could see the way the color washed across her face, and knew it would be the same all over her body. She would pinken as her body readied itself for him. Were he to reach for her under the table, he would find her hot and wet beneath his hands. He felt himself harden. He could not seem to get enough of her, no matter how often they sated each other. No matter how easily she came apart in his hands.

"I am no longer a princess," she said, her voice husky, a gleam of awareness in her magnificent eyes. "And you never use my name."

"I use your name," he contradicted her, smiling slightly, "in certain circumstances." He did not have to spell those circumstances out. Her flush deepened, as they both remembered the last time he'd called out her name, sometime before the dawn, when he'd been so deep inside of her he would have been happy to die there. She made him feel like a man, he realized. Not the soldier he had been, not the King he was now, but a man.

"There is more to life than sex," she said, and he saw a darkness pass through her eyes—some kind of shadow. But she blinked, and it was gone.

"Apparently not for you," he said lazily. "Apparently, you are bored with everything that happens outside our bed. One solution would be to make sure you never leave it."

"Promises, promises," she chided him, a gleam in her eyes. "Who would run the country if we spent all our time in bed?"

* * *

The man was insatiable, Lara thought.

And what was so astonishing was that she, who had always enjoyed the company of men but had certainly never felt *compelled* by them, was too.

He had her in the suites of hotels where they stayed while on royal engagements, her back up against the wall, his hand and mouth busy beneath her skirts. He seduced her on a speedboat as they made their way to one of the more remote clans, only accessible across a system of mountain lakes. There was no place he did not look at her with that dark passion, that promise, alive in his gray eyes. And no place where she did not immediately respond, no matter how inappropriate it might be.

It was lust, she told herself. And unexpected chemistry.

And she was no better.

She climbed astride him in the backseat of the plush limousine as the motorcade wove through the twisting streets of the capital city, rocking them both into bliss before a command appearance at the city opera. She had taken it upon herself to explore him in every room she could discover in the old castle—behind doors, on ancient chairs, under the fierce and disapproving glares of her ancestors high above in their glowering state portraits.

It was only lust, she thought. And lust was fine. Lust was allowed. Lust would fade. Though she could not help but note, every now and again as the summer wore on, that the more she touched him, the more she tasted him, the less she worried about the ways in which she might have lost herself in this strange little fairy-tale.

She was not an idiot. She did not, in truth, wish to govern, and doubted she would be any good at it, anyway. She would have no idea how one even went about it. Lara had no particular interest in politics, but she could, she realized, use the position she found herself in for good. There was no excuse for lying about a *castle*, of all places, feeling bored and put upon. How she would have slapped herself for even thinking such a thing, once upon a time, when her paycheck had had to last far too long and cover books and tuition as well as pay her rent! Appalled at herself, Lara began to involve herself in charity work—to get a sense of what her people, her subjects, her countrymen really needed.

And what she needed, too, if she was to stay here. If she was really to do this long-term. She pretended it was a life-style decision she was mulling over, like when she'd decided to stay in Colorado after college and make her life in Denver. She pretended it was a decision about a *location*, and about a *job*.

After all, fairy-tales weren't real. Not even this one.

"You are just like your father, may he rest in peace," an old woman told her as Lara toured one of the local hospitals, visiting the helpless and the needy, talking to the overworked staff. *I can help these people,* she had been thinking just moments before, as she'd tried to smile at a little girl gone bald from the cancer treatments, clearly the old woman's grandchild. *Maybe that's why I'm here.*

"I beg your pardon?" she asked, fighting to keep her smile in place as the old woman held on to her hands. It was not the physical contact she minded, she realized, but that wild intensity in the woman's eyes.

"He was a good man," the woman said, in the dialect of the upper mountains. "And a great king. I give thanks every day that you have returned to us, to bless us and help us prosper as your family has done for generations, no thanks to that evil woman who stole you away in the first place!"

And what could Lara say? It was hardly the place to argue—particularly with the grandmother of a sick child. And why did it seem as if the part of her that had defended Marlena for so long was simply...tired?

"Thank you," she said, fighting to keep her expression serene. "I hope I can live up to his memory."

Later that night, Lara met Adel at the start of a great ball to honor a dignitary whose name she had yet to commit to memory as she knew she should. The palace was alive with lights and Alakkul's most glamorous people were decked out in their finest clothes, all of it shining and sparkling. The palace gardens had been converted to a kind of wonderland for the evening, complete with a dance floor and little tables clustered in and around the flowering trees and geometrically shaped shrubberies. It was the end of August already. The twilight brought with it hints of the coming fall, the air was cool, and Lara felt a restlessness shiver through her, making her feel as if her skin was two sizes too small.

"You are fidgeting," Adel told her without altering his calm expression as they stood side by side to receive their guests. She did not have to look at him to know that he looked as he always did—so strong, so capable, his mouthwateringly male form displayed to perfection in the dark suit that clung to his every muscle and made his chest look like some kind of hard, male sculpture. He was mesmerizing. Still.

"It is just as well that you were raised since you were young to rule this place," she said, not thinking, letting the wildness that rolled inside of her have its way. "I would have made a terrible ruler. Perhaps you knew that. Perhaps my father did, too. Perhaps it is not sexism but practicality that governs you."

He did not reply. He shot her one of those dark, far-too-calm glances that made her breath catch, and something thick and heavy turn over into a knot in her gut. Then he returned to his duties, the endless greeting and acknowledging of guests, as if she had not spoken at all.

Later, he pulled her out on to the dance floor, and smiled slightly as he gazed down at her. His mouth was softer than usual, that hard line almost welcoming. The band swelled into a waltz as he held her in his arms, his hand in the small of her back seeming to beam heat and comfort directly into her skin through the silk of her gown, the hand holding hers so warm, so strong.

She did not know why she wanted, suddenly, to weep.

"What is the matter?" he asked in that quiet way of his, and she knew he was continuing the discussion from earlier, that nothing ever truly distracted a man of his focus.

"I do not know," she said, surprised to hear that she was whispering. She blinked, and tilted her head back to study his face. He only watched her, that boundless patience in his gray eyes—that calm readiness for whatever she might say, whenever she might say it to him.

"There is nothing you can tell me that will tarnish you in my eyes," he said in a low voice, sweeping her around the dance floor, his eyes on her as if nothing else existed. As if there was only the music, the palace, the low murmurs of the well-heeled guests, like a bubble around them. As if there was only this perfect, tiny jewel of a country, hidden away in remote mountains, beautiful in ways that hurt her soul. In the same way that he did.

And she understood, then, how easy it would be. To simply let go. To let him lead, as he did now, waltzing with the grace and mastery she had come to expect of him no matter what he did, his mouth in that enigmatic near-curve as he gazed down at her. It would be so easy to simply accept this life he'd given her. A country. A crown. And the endless delight of their explosive, uncontainable chemistry.

She need only forget herself. What she knew, who she was. She need only accept that her father was never the villain, but instead the misunderstood hero. She need only learn to think of her selfish, childish mother the way the Alakkulians obviously did—as the evil witch who had so destroyed their king with her string of lovers. The woman who had stolen away their princess. She need only erase all she'd believed to be true about her life, her world, *herself.*

And then she could have him, and all those dreams she'd longed for as a teenager would finally come true.

It would be as easy as breathing. As easy as letting him move her about the dance floor with all of his skill and grace. It would be so very, very easy—and she had done most of it already. She had become so concerned with turning herself into a proper queen—because she wanted his approval. She wanted that slow curve of his mouth that was only hers. She wanted the shine in his eyes that meant he was proud of her.

When had that happened? When had his opinion of her become more important to her than her own?

And why didn't that realization horrify her as she knew it ought to do?

"You look as if you have seen a ghost," Adel said softly, his lips so close to her ear that she shivered, feeling that low murmur in every part of her.

"Sometimes you make me feel as if I am one," she said, before she knew she meant to speak.

His head reared back slightly, and his eyes narrowed, but the song ended—and their ever-present aides interrupted them, prepared to usher the King to one table and the Queen to another.

"Duty calls," he murmured, holding on to her hand for a beat, then another, after the music had ended. Calling attention to the fact he had not let her go. "But we will return to this topic, Princess."

She had no doubt that they would.

And what did it say about her that anticipation was like honey in her veins, warming her, sweetening her, turning her into fire and need?

He stepped into her dressing room, and startled her as she reached to take down her hair, letting the heavy curls fall from the elaborate twist at the back of her head. She froze, meeting his gray gaze in the great mirror she stood before, its heavy gold and jeweled accents seeming to fade next to the raw power of the man who filled the doorway behind her.

Her heart began to speed up in her chest. Adel did not speak. He only held her gaze with his as he moved toward her, prowling across the thick carpet, all of that restrained power and force seeming to hum from his very skin. She did not look away, even when he came to a stop behind her, and traced a pattern along the sensitive skin at the nape of her neck. She did not look away when he bent his head and used his mouth instead of his hand, kissing and tasting a molten path from the tender place below her ear to the bared skin of her shoulder.

"You do not taste like a ghost," he said, a raw sort of urgency in his voice. She did not understand the darkness in his eyes then, but her body responded to it, as it always did.

"Neither do you," she said, turning her head and pressing her lips to his hard jaw.

"You do not feel like a ghost," he continued. She turned in his arms and pressed her breasts against his chest, then tested the shape of his arms beneath her hands.

His mouth claimed hers, insistent and demanding, and she gave herself over to this wicked sorcery, this dark delight, that only he could call forth in her. She slid the suit jacket from his wide shoulders, then busied herself with the buttons of his stiff dress shirt.

He growled with impatience, and shifted forward, lifting her up by her bottom and settling her back against the small table behind her—paying no heed to the small bottles and tubes he knocked out of his way. He reached down and pulled up the hem of her long gown, baring her to his sight. He let out something that sounded like a cross between a sigh and a groan, and then he reached down to hold her softness in his hand, feeling her molten heat, making her moan and move against him.

He made short work of the scrap of lace that concealed her

femininity, and then, with a few quick jerks at the fly of his own trousers, he was thrusting into her. Lara shuddered as he entered her, shattering around him, and coming back to find him watching her, those gray eyes intense. As if he could see deep into her, as if he knew the things she was afraid to face herself.

"Please…" she murmured, not knowing what she asked for, but he began to move.

He pulled her legs up, hooking them over his hips, as he thrust inside of her again and again. She felt the fire catch and then burn anew, bright and hot. He leaned down and took her mouth, possessing her, claiming her, making her nothing more than these sensations, these feelings. She burned for him, and he knew it, and she could not even bring herself to mind.

She could only fall apart once more, and hear his hoarse cry as he followed right behind her.

When she woke in the morning, wrapped around him in the great bed, she felt the seduction of this impossible fairy-tale pull at her yet again. She need only let go, and how hard could that be, she asked herself? Why did she fight it?

The slight chill in the morning air, blowing in through the open windows, reminded her that it was coming up hard on September already. She still felt as if it was June—or ought to be. She let her eyes drift closed again, inhaling Adel's intoxicating male scent, feeling his strength and heat beneath her. Where did the time go?

A thought occurred to her then, washing over her like a cold sweat. Her eyes snapped open. She counted back— tried to remember… But no, it was true. She had not had her monthly courses since she'd been in Denver. And she had not even thought about it.

But she thought about it now, sitting up straight in the bed, her heart in her throat and what remained of the fairy-tale shattering all around her like glass.

CHAPTER EIGHT

THREE days later, it was definitely September, Lara was most assuredly and unhappily pregnant, and more important, she'd finally woken up from the spell she'd been under ever since Adel Qaderi had appeared in that supermarket parking lot back in Denver. She was so wide awake it actually hurt.

She buckled herself into the plush seat in the private jet, willing herself to keep her emotions under control. She did not look out the window as the plane began to taxi down the runway. She did not glance back as the plane soared into the air, clearing the spires and parapets. She knew the country was spread out before her like a canvas, and she refused to indulge in one last look. She reached over and pulled the shade closed, as if she could block out the last few months as easily.

It was one thing to fall under Adel's sensual spell. She wasn't sure how she could have resisted him, once he'd looked at her with that passion simmering in his dark eyes. But it was something else entirely to bring another child into another loveless marriage. Hadn't she spent the whole of her life paying for her parents' marriage? Wasn't she still? Her hand crept over her still-flat belly. She could not do that to a child. *She would not do it.*

Her time in Alakkul might have felt like a dream, *her* dream, but it had also served to open up her eyes to the uncomfortable truth about her childhood—and her parents. She shut her eyes against another rush of emotion that threatened to suck her under. The truth was that her mother had stolen her away from her father, and had deliberately made Lara believe the worst of him. Another truth was that her father had not come to claim her, nor tell his side of the story before he died—not in twelve long years. Her mother had poisoned her against King Azat, all the while hiding the truth about the funds she'd taken and her own infidelities. The King, meanwhile, had sold his only child into a convenient marriage, to serve his own ends.

It didn't matter which parent she looked at, because the truth was blindingly clear to her either way. She had never been anything more than a pawn to either one of them. She certainly wouldn't inflict that same kind of life on her child. She'd die first.

Because as much as she'd claimed to hate King Azat to please her mother, and in many ways she had, the truth was that she'd yearned for a normal family like any other girl. She'd wanted a father *and* a mother.

And she'd missed Alakkul, too. And Adel, her first love. She did not know how she would manage to shove all those memories aside as she'd done before—but she knew she'd have to do it, somehow. The precious life she carried inside of her could never know the deep pangs of longing she felt for that cool, bright valley, tucked away in a forgotten corner of the world. Or the deeper yearning for a hard-faced man with eyes like rain and gentle hands. It would fade, she told herself. Someday, it would fade.

She let her head fall back against the cushioned headrest, and pretended she was unaware of the tears slipping from her eyes to trail across her cheeks. She would forget him. Again. The truth was that their chemistry had been so unexpected that she'd allowed it to confuse her for the whole long summer. It had only served to conceal the truth. Adel did not want *her*. He wanted King Azat's daughter. He wanted the throne of Alakkul. She could have been anyone, as long as he had gotten both of those things.

She was still nothing but a pawn. A strategy. A convenience he happened to be attracted to. And she knew with a deep certainty that her child deserved more. Much more.

Her heart might seem to break into more and more pieces with every mile she flew away from him, but she would lock that up with all her memories and put it away. She would do it, somehow. For her child, if not for herself.

Lara came awake slowly, confused. It took a moment or two to realize that the plane was on the ground, instead of in the air, and was rolling along the tarmac. Frowning, she pulled up the window shade nearest to her, but all she could see were streaks of rain against the window, and splotches of light in the dark. A terminal, perhaps—but where?

"Excuse me?" she called, twisting in her seat to seek out the hovering air hostess. "Where are we? What's going on?"

"It is nothing, Your Majesty," the woman said, her voice soothing, her smile calm. "The plane has been diverted to deal with a slight mechanical issue. A hotel suite has been secured for your use, and you should be on your way again in the morning."

Lara was still half-asleep, perhaps—or just confused in general, so she almost forgot to ask, again, where they'd landed. The nervous tension she'd felt disappeared when the woman named a small Baltic country far to the north and west of Alakkul, and she realized that she'd suspected the plane had simply returned her to Alakkul while she'd slept. She told herself she was delighted to be wrong.

There was not much to see of the country so late at night. She was escorted into a waiting car, and whisked away to an elegant hotel in a city center not twenty minutes away from the air field. Lara felt suspended—at loose ends—and knew it was because she had to stop here and *think* about what she was doing. That had not been her plan. She'd wanted to be firmly back on American soil, deeply ensconced in her old, comfortable little life again before she had to think about the ramifications of her abrupt departure from the new life she'd been living all summer.

She had not even spoken to Adel. She had not given him any warning. She had simply seen the royal physician, confirmed what she'd known must be true, and had plotted her immediate escape.

But as the elevator took her toward the penthouse suite, one more luxury she would forgo the moment she returned to the real world, she could not help but ask herself if what she was doing right now was any different from what Marlena had done so many years before. Was it different because the child she carried was not yet born? Wouldn't the child be the heir to the throne just as Lara had been? Wouldn't this same cycle play itself out all over again? Could she really be responsible for inflicting this much pain on her own baby?

She had no answers. And, as she stepped into the suite, she took a deep breath, noted the expensive displays of flowers and the subtly elegant furnishings, and realized—with a start and a leap of something like anticipation in her belly— that she was out of time.

Because a man stood there, half concealed by the shadows deep in the room, watching her approach as if he'd summoned her.

Adel.

He could not remember being so angry before. Ever. Because he could not recall ever caring this much—about anything.

His gaze tracked her as she walked toward him, then stopped. She flinched as she recognized that she was not alone. She looked tired—dark smudges beneath her eyes and her skin too pale in the warm glow of the lamps that lit the large room. He was so furious it was all he could do to keep it locked inside of him. To keep from shouting at her. To keep from demanding she tell him that this was not really happening—that she would not leave him like this, taking so much with her. Surely she could not really do this. Surely it was a mistake—a misunderstanding.

"Be easy," he said quietly, but even he could hear the lash in his voice. "I will not put my hands on you when I am this angry."

Her gaze flared into a bright blue blaze, as if he'd deeply offended her. But how could he have done?

"I take it this is all some complicated charade," she bit out. "There is nothing wrong with the plane, is there? There is no mechanical failure!"

"That rather depends on your definition," he replied icily. "I would categorize an abdicating queen as a failure of the highest degree."

She let out a small noise, too rough to be a sigh, and turned her head away. She sank down on one of the butter-soft leather couches, but did not seem to see it. She wrapped her arms around her torso, and still, did not look at him. Something hard and heavy, like a stone, fell through him.

She was really doing this. She had done it, and he had only managed to engineer this stop at the last moment. She was leaving him, and taking his child with him. *His child.*

He was a man of action, of deeds and solutions, and he could only stand there, frozen. What had she done to him? How had he been reduced to this? Why could he think of nothing save how to comfort her?

"I cannot do this," she said in a low voice. "I gave you your throne. What else can you possibly want?"

"I want you," he said, the words torn from him. Painful. "My queen. My *wife.*"

"Your pawn," she countered, her head whipping back around so that her gaze could meet his. He was shocked by the pain he saw there, the darkness. "Do you know something,

Adel? I have been the pawn of one king or another since the day I was born. I am sick of it."

"You are not a pawn," he began.

"How can you say that with a straight face?" she demanded. She surged back to her feet. "Did you chase me across the world because you liked my personality? Because you thought about *me* at all? No—you wanted what only my particular parentage could give you. My special genetic make-up. If that does not make me a pawn, then I do not know the meaning of the word."

"You do not understand," he said, gritting out the words, because he did not like the picture she painted—and yet, given the option, he would do it all over again in exactly the same way. If he knew that, why should it eat at him? "I had no choice in these things, but that has nothing to do with what is between us now. What was always between us, even when we were young."

"There is nothing between us." Her voice was flat, her eyes unreadable. Like a stranger's. "It was the madness of summer, nothing more. I gave you what you wanted. Now it's your turn to return the favor."

"What is it you want?" he asked, although he knew what she would say, and she did not disappoint him. She was so cold, and yet that dark anger shone in her silver-blue eyes and hinted at the turmoil beneath, the fire he knew burned within her.

"My freedom," she cried at him.

"Perhaps that can be arranged," he said, then prowled closer to her, noting the way her pulse jumped in her throat, and she swallowed—nervously, he thought. He moved even closer, making her tilt her head back to keep looking him in the eye. "But I have one question about this freedom of yours."

"What?" It was as close to a growl as he'd heard come from her lips, and under other circumstances he might have found it amusing. But not tonight. Not here. Not when his whole life hung in the balance.

"What of the child?" he asked.

Lara felt herself pale, and thought she might have swayed on her feet—but then temper took over. She shook off the urge to collapse into some kind of decorative swoon, and glared at him.

"That doctor had no business telling you something private!" she hissed. "So much for confidentiality!"

"He is the royal physician," Adel snapped. "Last I checked, he serves at *my* pleasure. Of course he told me—especially after I tore the palace apart trying to find out where and why you'd gone. How could you think to keep your condition from me?"

"How could you think I would tell you?" she threw at him, hearing the wildness in her own voice. The years of baggage. "So you could have one more bargaining chip to hold over my head?"

A muscle worked in his jaw. His gray eyes seemed to chill, and then turned to some kind of steel. Lara shivered, but she could not understand herself. Why should some reckless part of her want to comfort him? Even now? What was the matter with her?

"So this, then, is what you think of me," he said in that low voice, and she realized, perhaps for the first time, that he was not as in control as he appeared. That the clenched jaw and deliberately controlled voice were smoke screens. That he was as furious as she'd ever seen him.

"It is nothing more than the truth," she said, bravely, because the understanding that he was not the cold, controlled creature she'd imagined made her tremble deep inside. It changed everything, she thought—and yet, could change nothing. She could not let it.

"This is who I am to you," he continued. "After all that has passed between us."

"You mean sex," she threw at him, heedless of the danger. Her temper—fused tightly to a growing feeling of despair— threatened to swamp her completely. "Threats and compulsion and sex—that is all that has ever passed between us!"

"I love you." The words were like a slap—thrown down, harsh and abrupt, to lie between them. There was an expression she did not understand in his dark eyes, and a rush of joy she refused to acknowledge in her own heart.

"That is a lie." Her throat hurt, as if too much lodged there that she could not bear to say.

"I have loved you from the start," he said with a certain dignity, a quiet insistence. "From the first moment I saw you, when you were little more than a girl. I have loved you my whole life. Nothing has changed that. Nothing could."

Oh, how her treacherous heart yearned to believe him! But she knew him—more than she wanted to, and better than she should. She knew his ruthlessness, his focus. In bed and in his pursuit of whatever else he wanted. Look at how quickly he had turned her from defiance to purring contentment in his arms! Look at the way her body warmed for him even now!

"You will say anything," she said, appalled to hear the catch in her voice, but unable to stop it, much less the hot tears that followed. "*Do* anything. Do you think I don't know that? You told me so yourself. This is who you are. The man who cannot compromise. The man who is not modern."

"Lara—"

"I cannot do this again!" she cried, and there was nothing held back anymore, nothing hidden. She looked at him and she saw all the betrayals and disappointments of her youth. All the times she'd known, somehow, that Marlena was not telling her the truth. All the lonely days and nights spent waiting for Azat to come and claim her, to let her know she was worth something to him. Worth fighting for.

"There is no *again*," Adel said fiercely. "There is only you. Me. This child. I cannot change the circumstances that have brought us here, Lara, but how can you doubt—"

"I won't do it," she threw at him. "I won't subject my own child to this endless tug of war, this game with no end. I will not have this baby grow up wondering what she's worth, and why, and have her squabbled over like a piece of meat in the market. Not this child!"

"This child will be loved," he said, in that wild voice, low and throbbing. Uncontrolled. "Celebrated and adored."

"Yes, far away from thrones and politics. And you."

The silence seemed to hum between them. Lara was aware, suddenly, of the rain beating against the windows, and her own tears wet on her cheeks. She dashed at them with her fists, her breathing too fast, too hard. And all the while, Adel gazed at her, his beautiful, hard face open in a way it had never been before—*shattered*, a small voice inside of her whispered.

As if she'd destroyed him. As if she—or anyone—could have that power.

She wanted to turn away, but she could not make herself do it. She wanted to go to him, to press her lips against the uncompromising lines of his jaw, his brow. She did not do that, either. Could not let herself.

"I told you I loved you," he said, as if from a great distance. "I have never loved anyone else in my life. Only you. Always you."

"Prove it," she heard herself say—harsh and fast. Before she could think better of it, or change her mind. "Let me go."

She thought the bleakness in his eyes might have killed her right there, on the spot. She felt it pierce her heart, and shoot like fire through her veins, making her stomach lurch. She gasped for breath.

But Adel merely bowed his head slightly, as if the anguish she could see in his face was nothing at all.

"If that is what you want," he said, his voice the barest thread of sound, and yet it still seemed like a lash against her flesh. "Then it is yours."

And then Lara watched him turn and walk out of the hotel door, leaving her, just as she'd claimed she'd wanted.

So why, when the door closed behind him and the room was empty of everything save the rain against the windows, did she feel as if part of her had just died?

CHAPTER NINE

SHE walked back into the palace like a warrior, proud and strong, and Adel felt his heart stop in his chest.

Then begin to beat, hard. Something inside of him, granite and cold, began to ease as she stalked across the great marble floor of what had once been the throne room and was now the antechamber to his office.

"I did not expect to see you again," he said, standing in the doorway between the two rooms, his arms folded across his chest. It had been two days. He knew, intellectually, that those forty-eight hours had been no longer than any other set of forty-eight hours, but it had not felt that way.

He had believed she was lost to him. Forever.

"I did not expect you to give up and slink away like a whipped puppy," she threw at him as she closed the distance between them, going immediately for the jugular. He should not admire that as he did. She should not arouse him, with her temper and her daring. He should be furious that she had turned on him, run from him—and on some level he was. But more than that, he wanted her. He wanted her, and she was here, and she was glorious.

And his.

"You told me to set you free, Princess," he drawled. Surely she had come back in all ways, or why would she have come back at all? "I was only following your orders."

She came to a stop before him, her remarkable eyes a mix

of bravado and something else, something that made him long to touch her. It took all he had to keep from doing so.

Not yet, he thought. Not just yet.

"Since when do you listen to what I want?" she asked, a slight frown between her eyes. "I cannot recall a single instance of you ever doing so, in all the time I've known you."

"I cannot follow this conversation," he replied, his tone silky, his attention on her lush mouth. "I am a bully if I do not listen to you, and a whipped puppy if I do?"

She did not answer him. She only gazed at him for a long moment, her full mouth soft, her eyes big. Adel could feel the tension between them, the kick and the spark. He could see the truth of it reflected in the way she caught her breath, the way her body swayed toward his as if of its own volition.

Mine, he thought, deep inside. Like a perfect note played on a traditional *balalaika*, low and true.

"You said you loved me." She said it so matter-of-factly, yet he could still hear the question. The uncertainty.

"I do." And then he could not help but touch her, reaching across the space he did not want between them to hold her soft cheek in his hand. She shivered slightly, and then leaned into it, like a cat. "And I suspect you must feel the same, or you would not be here. You would have gone on to America. You would not have returned."

"It seems I cannot stay away," she said softly.

"Nor should you," he said. "You are the Queen, Lara. You are my wife. This is your home."

Lara blew out a breath, as a shadow moved over her face. "I do not want what my parents had," she said, her silver-blue eyes so serious it made Adel ache. "I refuse to do to this child what was done to me. Or to you. I refuse."

"Stay with me, Princess," he said softly, raising his other hand to hold her face between them, looking deep into her eyes, into their future. "We will make the world whatever we wish it to be, together."

* * *

Once again, Lara stood out on the terrace high in the mountains and looked out over the Alakkulian Valley. It sparkled in the bright morning light, the chill of the coming autumn already moving in from the higher elevations, bringing a sharper kind of light and a certain crispness to the air. She pulled her thick robe tighter over her torso and snuggled into it, flexing her toes against the cold stones beneath her.

She felt...alive. More alive than she had ever felt before.

Because she had chosen, finally. For the first time since Adel had appeared before her in that far-off parking lot, as if conjured out of the June afternoon, *she* had decided.

She had sat in that anonymous hotel room for what seemed like weeks, unable to process both what had happened and her own reaction to it. She'd wanted to die. She'd felt as if part of her had, as every moment stretched out and seemed to last forever, all of them resoundingly, painfully empty of Adel. She had not understood how she could yearn for him so much, *hunger* for him. How his absence could feel like a missing limb. How she could want him near her as much for the calm, quiet steadiness of his presence as for the desire he could stir in her with a single glance.

But then she'd realized that this time, it was up to her. He had let her go. His doing so had shocked her, but it had also freed her, as she'd wanted.

And once she was free, and could choose to be anywhere, Lara had realized that there was only once place on earth that called to her. Only one place on earth she could feel like herself anymore.

How had that happened? When had it happened? How had she put all of her past aside without even noticing it? Because while every word she'd thrown at him in that hotel room had been true, the truth was, there was no point being free, or strong, or *alive*, without him. None of that held any appeal.

She heard the French doors open behind her. She smiled slightly. They had hardly slept—reaching for each other again and again in the night. Re-learning each other. Revelling in her return, and renouncing their separation in the most intimate way possible. She leaned back into the warm, solid wall of his chest as he moved behind her, marveling at the way her body readied itself for his touch. Her knees felt weak. Her core melted. She even felt heat behind her eyes.

He was hers. He loved her.

Standing in his arms, looking out at the beautiful country of her birth, Lara realized that finally, *finally*, she'd found the home she'd been looking for all of her life.

She turned to look at him. That hard face. That uncompromising mouth. That tough, warrior's body. And all of it hers, forever.

Because she'd been given the choice—a real choice this time—and she'd chosen him.

"I love you," she whispered, though it felt like a shout, a howl, that could be heard from mountain to mountain across the great valley. His mouth curved.

"So you have showed me," he said quietly. He let his hand trace a path down her body, slipping it inside her robe to her abdomen, where he placed it over the child they'd made. The child they would raise together, in this country they would rule.

And maybe, just maybe, just for them, if they worked hard enough to make it happen, the fairy tales would come true. Exactly as they'd dreamed together, so many years ago.

* * * * *

CLASSIC

Quintessential, modern love stories
that are romance at its finest.

You can find more information on upcoming Harlequin® titles,
free excerpts and more at www.HarlequinInsideRomance.com.

REQUEST YOUR
FREE BOOKS!

2 FREE NOVELS PLUS
2 FREE GIFTS!

YES! Please send me 2 FREE Harlequin Presents® novels and my 2 FREE gifts (gifts are worth about $10). After receiving them, if I don't wish to receive any more books, I can return the shipping statement marked "cancel." If I don't cancel, I will receive 6 brand-new novels every month and be billed just $4.30 per book in the U.S. or $4.99 per book in Canada. That's a saving of at least 14% off the cover price! It's quite a bargain! Shipping and handling is just 50¢ per book in the U.S. and 75¢ per book in Canada.* I understand that accepting the 2 free books and gifts places me under no obligation to buy anything. I can always return a shipment and cancel at any time. Even if I never buy another book, the two free books and gifts are mine to keep forever.

106/306 HDN FERQ

Name	(PLEASE PRINT)
Address	Apt. #
City	State/Prov.	Zip/Postal Code

Signature (if under 18, a parent or guardian must sign)

Mail to the **Reader Service:**
IN U.S.A.: P.O. Box 1867, Buffalo, NY 14240-1867
IN CANADA: P.O. Box 609, Fort Erie, Ontario L2A 5X3

Not valid for current subscribers to Harlequin Presents books.

**Are you a current subscriber to Harlequin Presents books
and want to receive the larger-print edition?
Call 1-800-873-8635 or visit www.ReaderService.com.**

* Terms and prices subject to change without notice. Prices do not include applicable taxes. Sales tax applicable in N.Y. Canadian residents will be charged applicable taxes. Offer not valid in Quebec. This offer is limited to one order per household. All orders subject to credit approval. Credit or debit balances in a customer's account(s) may be offset by any other outstanding balance owed by or to the customer. Please allow 4 to 6 weeks for delivery. Offer available while quantities last.

Your Privacy—The Reader Service is committed to protecting your privacy. Our Privacy Policy is available online at www.ReaderService.com or upon request from the Reader Service.

We make a portion of our mailing list available to reputable third parties that offer products we believe may interest you. If you prefer that we not exchange your name with third parties, or if you wish to clarify or modify your communication preferences, please visit us at www.ReaderService.com/consumerschoice or write to us at Reader Service Preference Service, P.O. Box 9062, Buffalo, NY 14269. Include your complete name and address.

*Lucy Flemming and Ross Mitchell shared a magical,
sexy Christmas weekend together six years ago.
This Christmas, history may repeat itself when they find
themselves stranded in a major snowstorm...
and alone at last.*

Read on for a sneak peek from
IT HAPPENED ONE CHRISTMAS
by Leslie Kelly.

Available December 2011, only from Harlequin® Blaze™.

EYEING THE GRAY, THICK SKY through the expansive wall of
windows, Lucy began to pack up her photography gear.
The Christmas party was winding down, only a dozen or so
people remaining on this floor, which had been transformed
from cubicles and meeting rooms to a holiday funland. She
smiled at those nearest to her, then, seeing the glances at her
silly elf hat, she reached up to tug it off her head.

Before she could do it, however, she heard a voice. A
deep, male voice—smooth and sexy, and so not Santa's.

"I appreciate you filling in on such short notice. I've
heard you do a terrific job."

Lucy didn't turn around, letting her brain process what
she was hearing. Her whole body had stiffened, the hairs on
the back of her neck standing up, her skin tightening into
tiny goose bumps. Because that voice sounded so familiar.
Impossibly familiar.

It can't be.

"It sounds like the kids had a great time."

Unable to stop herself, Lucy began to turn around,
wondering if her ears—and all her other senses—were
deceiving her. After all, six years was a long time, the mind

could play tricks. What were the odds that she'd bump into *him,* here? And today of all days. December 23.

Six years exactly. Was that really possible?

One look—and the accompanying frantic thudding of her heart—and she knew her ears and brain were working just fine. Because it was *him.*

"Oh, my God," he whispered, shocked, frozen, staring as thoroughly as she was. "Lucy?"

She nodded slowly, not taking her eyes off him, wondering why the years had made him even more attractive than ever. It didn't seem fair. Not when she'd spent the past six years thinking he must have started losing that thick, golden-brown hair, or added a spare tire to that trim, muscular form.

No.

The man was gorgeous. Truly, without-a-doubt, mouth-wateringly handsome, every bit as hot as he'd been the first time she'd laid eyes on him. She'd been twenty-two, he one year older.

They'd shared an amazing holiday season.

And had never seen one another again.

Until now.

Find out what happens in
IT HAPPENED ONE CHRISTMAS
by Leslie Kelly.
Available December 2011, only from Harlequin® Blaze™

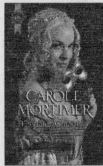